At home, the 17-year-old author still lives with both of his parents, his father, a Cambridge PhD graduate working as a Methodist Minister; and his mother, a Science teacher. He also has three older siblings.

When he isn't fantasising about conspiracy theories, listening to or playing his own music or reading novels, he is studying hard for his A-levels in French, Politics and English Literature.

Dedicated to God, my family, all those who have supported me and all those who will continue to support me throughout my life.

Gabriel Dedji

THE ESCAPE

A Tale of Change and Revolution

To Loyle Carner,
Thank you for being an inspiration.
Signed: G Dedji

AUSTIN MACAULEY PUBLISHERS™

LONDON · CAMBRIDGE · NEW YORK · SHARJAH

A CIP catalogue record for this title is available from the British Library.

ISBN 9781528930994 (Paperback)
ISBN 9781528931007 (Hardback)
ISBN 9781528966481 (ePub e-book)

www.austinmacauley.com

First Published (2019)
Austin Macauley Publishers Ltd
25 Canada Square
Canary Wharf
London
E14 5LQ

To begin with, I must thank God: my inspiration. Without his divine presence and guidance, I question whether this book would have arrived to this stage or even have been written at all. I thank God for my family: the people who have been everything for me. I cannot thank my parents enough for the never-ending support they provide for me despite the fact that we, more often than not, don't see each other eye to eye artistically. I express my gratitude for them and my siblings because they have taught me to keep my feet on the ground as I grow tall with a head in the clouds.

Finally, but also quite importantly, there is no way in which I can even begin to name all of the people, some unaware of this current accomplishment, who have moved me to continue the writing of this book simply because of their kindness towards me and my family. Your gifts of food, cards and your constant need to ensure that we are in good health, out of the goodness of your hearts, have all been pieces of inspiration and motivational delight through sleepless nights.

Prologue
Chapter 1

The time is 14:57. Humphrey Anit, a language teacher, is taking care of a class that is full of students who do not listen.

Humphrey Anit was a good teacher. He was a man of Indian descent, but he had clearly spent most of his life in England. In the eyes of the students, he was seen as a gentle giant due to the fact he was around 6'4". Humphrey was also frustrated. He sat at the front of the class observing the ongoing mayhem. Usually the class would misbehave until Humphrey told them to be quiet and sit down. They usually listened to him and respected him, because he listened to his students and respected them. Today, however, his students had gone crazy. They were wild as they ran around the room rampant (all 26 of them). He tried helplessly to control his *'learning family'*. The term made him sick. In other schools, the term 'form group' was used. The term *'learning family'* indicated that a learning guide had some sort of moral responsibility for these students apart from doing the register, telling them off and occasionally praising them. Despite the fact that he didn't really have any moral responsibilities, Humphrey took it upon himself to make sure every student he taught felt happy in the school. Humphrey was an angel for all the students: a true Godsend. So it was a shame that he was keeping the secret that he was leaving the students at the end of the year.

Two boys, one of them Congolese and the other English, caused a kerfuffle as a class discussion progressed into an argument and others chimed in too. Another boy sat in the corner of the classroom, throwing pens and scrunched up pieces of paper at people across the classroom for no apparent reason. He hid and ducked under his chair as people proclaimed that they would beat up the person who had thrown something at them. Three Kurdish boys shoved each other around and kicked each other for a £1 scramble. Another group of girls screamed as they caught up on the latest gossip. This classroom was wild. A girl named Violet although innocent and sweet was incredibly annoyed at Maverick—the mischievous troublemaker of the class—for taking her pencil case and water bottle. She chased him around the classroom, and they threw chairs and tables around in the process. The room was in disarray, and the noise was deafening.

There he was: Mr Anit's favourite student. He was a young boy who was far from well behaved but nowhere near the troublemaking standards that were set by Maverick. Today he decided to refrain from taking part in any unruly behaviour. He looked at Mr Anit's face and comprehended his frustration and tiredness. Mr Anit couldn't wait to go home and see his wife and his son. The boy had a light bulb moment. He took a small keyboard looking instrument out of his bag. He connected a whistle to the keyboard-like instrument and blew into it whilst playing the keyboard with his right hand. Suddenly, music started to play. The sound was peculiar. The melody was a syncopated and slowed down combination of traditional afro beat and jazz (so out of place for the scenario). It was almost musically perfect, but it sounded as if it was missing the percussion of Tony Allen or another similar musician (which was extremely hard to find). The source of the sound was alien: like the hybrid of a harmonica, accordion and recorder. Everyone stopped their noise. They were all mesmerised. The boy was like a pied piper, using music as a mystic tool leading his audience to quiet. He ended the piece with a perfect cadence. There was a silence for a few seconds. It wasn't an awkward silence. It was a silence that contained the amazement of the class at this odd instrument. The

Congolese boy who was arguing with his English friend was intrigued.

"What other songs can you play?" he asked in excitement.

The boy with the melodica thought to himself. He then thought of the perfect song. He played a song off of Kendrick Lamar's newest album. This instrumental was a simple melody built off of three notes, but multiple students smiled as they recognised the tune. The buzzer went.

"Tuck your chairs in and have a good day,"

Mr Anit announced to the class as they left.

The students from the learning family left swiftly and orderly although some left their chairs untucked.

"Bon travail. C'était excellent. Merci beaucoup,"

Mr Anit told his favourite student.

"Ce n'était rien. J'aime jouer de la musique et je ne pouvais pas voir mon meilleur prof mécontent," the student replied.

Prologue
Chapter 2

Mr Anit's favourite student: the boy with the melodica is tired thus has decided to leave his friends and go home alone.

This young boy had spent his entire life in London, but his family was from a country in the continent of Africa. He came from a good household, and his parents always taught him to aspire for the best. The student did listen to his parents in terms of aiming for the best, but his parents believed that the best meant maths, science and anything that fell under those two. However, this boy was not a scientist or a mathematician. He was a dreamer. He was a writer. He was a poet. In his world, his future consisted of changing the world to be a better place through his gifts of writing and music composition. He would daydream about his future constantly. He did so as he walked home. He nearly hit a speeding ambulance as he crossed the road.

The name of the ambulance driver was James Cooder. He hurried down the road, parting traffic at will to arrive at a scene of injury to save someone's life. James and his work-partner, Cathie who sat next to him in the ambulance were both frustrated when they had to stop abruptly for the young boy who wasn't paying attention whilst crossing the road. They made it to the crime scene, but it was too late. A man lay on the floor with a knife in his stomach and two men were running away in opposite directions. A woman and her seven-year-old son, presumably the family of the man, stood holding hands, crying for someone to save the man's life. Nothing could be done.

Chapter 1

Rasharn White and his friends are relaxing during their summer holiday. They bump into Emmanuel Akinyemi and his friends who robbed Rasharn's twin brother a month ago. Rasharn has a weapon on him. The encounter happens around 15:30 in a rough area known for gang violence.

"I promise you, you will die right here!" shouted Rasharn with a thundering voice, full of a vicious anger.

A lightning punch swiftly landed on Rasharn's face creating a crunching sound in his jaw. The belief that lightning never strikes twice was disproved as several of Rasharn's friends delivered powerful blows not only to Rasharn's enemy, Emmanuel, but Emmanuel's whole entourage in an act of spontaneous retaliation. Emmanuel and his friends fought back violently in self-defence. A battle broke out between both groups. They were a group of uncontrollable lions, tackling each other furiously for their own pride and self-confidence; pouncing on each other in vain as neither side would ever win. The fighting was accompanied by cries of aggression. Rasharn grabbed one of his opponents and swung him to the floor. The opponent quickly regained balance and spat on Rasharn's face, his saliva was coloured scarlet red with blood. This was the ultimate act of disrespect. Rasharn was then punched in the stomach before his anger could evolve. The two traded jabs at each other's face, pushing their bodies to the physical limit, like professional boxers. The other delinquents involved in the conflict were distracted by their fray.

Emmanuel, the initial victim of Rasharn's fury, swung a boy to the floor and ran to help his friend like a mounted knight, arrogantly coming to the rescue so he could bring his side to victory. He ran behind Rasharn, seized him then threw him to the floor. Emmanuel, filled with arrogance and violent adrenaline, stomped repeatedly on Rasharn, with his size 12 boots, as if he was about to dig him straight into a hole in the floor 6 feet deep. One of Rasharn's friends lunged at Emmanuel out of nowhere as if he had flown out of the chamber of a cannon. Both of them fell to the floor and wrestled with each other to get back on their feet. Rasharn stood back up. His face was bruised, his eye was black and his body looked weak with pain. Shouts of profanity were amplified out of his mouth whilst everyone watched, and he took a machete out of a rip on the inside of his coat. They were standing on the back roads of a rough area in London. The area was usually empty due to the fear of parents for their own life and their children's lives because of gang violence. Today at this moment in time, a small crowd, five or six women strong, had amassed in the distance. The women were from some nearby council flats and had come out to see where all the noise was coming from. They were barely able to distinguish faces, but an enormous machete was recognisable even from the distance. Now they were holding their phones, ready to call the police.

BANG

The noise was ear piercing. It sounded like a gunshot. The hooligans looked around with searching eyes to see who had been shot and where the shot came from. Remel, the young man who had lunged at Emmanuel, looked at the sky. Remel, who was not only a gang affiliate but also a student gifted in physics, recognised the circle-shaped cloud in the sky: it was the result of an aircraft breaking the sound barrier. *Not a plane*, he thought (atypically to everyone else around him in consideration of the situation). His thoughts were disrupted by an explosive flying kick to the stomach of Rasharn—who was still wielding a knife—from Emmanuel. Despite the fact that Rasharn was able to stay standing, he was disconcerted, winded and his machete had fallen to the ground. Remel hastily ran towards the weapon and picked it up without thinking. One of the delinquent boys grabbed Emmanuel and put him in a headlock. The boy struggled to keep Emmanuel in his grasp. They both wrestled for control.

"Stab him! Do it!"

The boy screamed with so much desperation that Remel could only do as he was told. He was about to strike.

Out of nowhere, music started to be played. The sound was peculiar. The melody was a syncopated and slowed down combination of traditional afro beat and jazz (so out of place for the scenario). It was almost musically perfect, but it sounded as if it was missing the percussion of Tony Allen or another similar musician (which was extremely hard to find). The source of the sound was alien: like the hybrid of a harmonica, accordion and recorder. Remel and the other young boys paused. Their bodies froze in their stances. Their eyes surveyed the area in search of the source of the mystic sound. The women watching the climax of the brawl were now calmer than before and less curious; they put their phones away. Remel spotted a man no further than 20 yards away from him with a black iron mask. Only half of his face (from his head to his upper lip) was covered. The iron-masked man was the source of the tune. Remel was in awe. All the other boys looked at the man. He had a skinny frame which was decorated with slim-fit, black trousers and a white buttoned shirt. The man wore a long, black overcoat that stopped just above his knees. He was extremely tall compared to Remel and the other boys who were staring at him. The man ended his song with a perfect cadence. He then took his melodica and clipped it to his back confidently. His muscle memory was obvious: he performed this basic action often. He took the whistle off of his melodica and placed it in the pocket of his coat as he walked towards the boys who had previously been in a fight that would put them all in prison for murder under the act of joint enterprise.

"Drop the weapon," the iron-masked man spoke softly, but his words resonated with the young boys and Remel in particular. It was as if the man not only spoke to the hooligans, but he was simultaneously communicating with them telepathically.

"Go home."

The iron-masked man still spoke softly, but this time his voice had a more imperative tone.

"Who are you?" asked Remel inquisitively.

"Go and you'll find me," the man commanded.

The boys followed his order, and they all made their way home to their houses and council flats with a feeling of peace in their bodies and no urge to fight. Remel on the other hand felt a sense of dissatisfaction and curiosity as to what the man meant. It was all so strange.

Around 20 minutes later, Remel walked home alone. He was slightly perplexed by the events that had just taken place. When he reached his house, his hands fiddled in his coat pocket to reach his keys. He found them, but he could also feel a small piece of paper in his pocket. He took it out of his pocket and he saw printed writing on it. The words read: 'King Keys, The Perpetually Pensive Poet. Read Jeremiah 29:11'.

Chapter 2

Remel Brathwaite is at home, confused and trying to understand what had happened.

Remel read the paper several times over whilst standing at the door. The phrasing was odd. After the eighth time reading the paper, he placed it back in his trouser pocket and walked into his house. He was hit with the smell of his mum's cooking. The air was flavoured with plantain and fried chicken. The smell gave his heart a sense of warmth, even though his thoughts were unfocussed. He took off his dirtied jacket and placed his shoes in his shoe room then went to the bathroom. He stared at himself in the mirror. His hair, cut into a low temple fade, was rough and messy. He had a scar on his forehead and a bruise on his cheek, however this was not what he was looking for. He washed the dirt off of his palms and the blood off of his knuckles. The blood took a while to clear, but eventually, his hands were clean of evidence of the fight. He dried his hands, placed them in his pocket and took the piece of paper out. The words read: 'King Keys, The Perpetually Pensive Poet. Read Jeremiah 29:11'. He had already read it numerous times, and each time, more questions clouded his head.

Understanding was the only cure for Remel's state of confusion. He made his way to his room and examined his bookshelf. His attention was caught by a small book at the top of the shelf. It was a book, and it was small and brown so it was extremely ironic that it intimidated Remel. There was a clear dichotomy between the boy who was ready to murder someone he barely knew because his friend told him to and the young man who stood there almost in tears in front of his bookshelf. He picked up the book. Another book dropped. Remel looked down at the floor and stared at a book titled: 'Boys Don't Cry'. He almost laughed at the irony as a teardrop fell on the cover. The book remained on the floor, because Remel didn't feel as if he had time. The book in his hand demanded urgency. The title of this book was 'The Holy Bible'. Remel could only stare at the book in awe as a surge of nostalgia rushed through him. He remembered the days he spent at church, not only in Sunday services but also during the week, taking part in youth clubs with all of his best friends. Then it hit him. One memory that he had worked so hard to repress escaped from the inner depths of his mind. Remel was seven when his father died from a fatal stabbing. His mother didn't know that Remel could remember that day. In fact, his mother was nearly correct. He had worked so hard to imprison the feelings and memories.

His heart was pounding as he remembered the adrenaline taking over his body when his dad lay on the floor dying. He remembered the sight of his father shouting at two young gang members to stop fighting. His father heroically tried to jump in the middle of the two before they could take each other's lives. The single teardrop which fell on the book 'Boys Don't Cry' was nothing compared to the Niagara Falls reconstruction Remel was now displaying on his face. The echo of the news headline after his father's death still haunted him.

"Man dies as a result of gang fight."

The woman presenting the news unsympathetically explained with an emotionless expression.

They didn't criminalise his father by twisting up the story, but they didn't explain that he wasn't part of the violence. They didn't explain that Remel's father was a hero. They didn't explain that he was a church worship leader, an organ donor and a loving father. Remel soaked up the ocean on his face with his sleeve and averted his attention to his Bible. He went to the contents page and searched for Jeremiah. He opened up the page and looked for chapter 29. He then looked for the eleventh verse of the chapter. 'For I know the plans that I have for you, says the LORD, plans for peace and not for evil, to give you a future and a hope'.

When his father was alive, Remel was proud to wear the badge of being a Christian. Even though he was young, he knew all about his faith. He was a saint. When his father died, he was too small, so the obvious questions that were normally asked when a close one died like: 'If there were a God why would he let this happen?', 'Why did it happen?' or 'Why couldn't it be prevented?' were too overwhelming for him to answer. He and his mother took bereavement counselling at the church that his dad went to. During the first and only session of counselling they went to, the preacher handed them a piece of paper with a bible verse printed on it. The verse was Jeremiah 29 verse 11. After reading it in their heads, Remel and his mother stayed silent. The minister looked in the eyes of Remel and his mother before letting the words 'everything happens for a reason' come out of his mouth. Remel's mother stood up, left and Remel followed because he had to. One thing you can never do is tell a bereaved person that everything happens for a reason. That was the last time Remel went to church.

Over time, Remel started to forget about God and the church. By the time he was 14, he labelled himself agnostic. He started living his life as he wished and stopped ignoring the devil on his shoulder. He also stopped avoiding bad company and trouble. If there was a God—he said—she or he had given him the ability and freewill to do what he liked so his behaviour was a sign of appreciation for the way he had been created. 'YOLO' and 'Carpe Diem' were his mottos, but he knew what he could and couldn't do. His parents had raised him to be a good man regardless of what religion. At the age of 15, Remel discovered the term 'nihilist' and adopted the label without fully understanding what it meant. Now at the age of 18—almost 19—with a Bible in his hand, Remel wondered what he really was.

After an hour of uncontrolled and emotional reflection on his life, Remel picked 'Boys Don't Cry' off of the floor and placed it back on the bookshelf in return for a book called

'Philosophical Terms for Beginners' whilst he still held on to the Bible in his other hand. The book was immaculate and untouched. It was supposed to be used for revision, but it was unused due to the fact that he constantly had full marks in his in-class philosophy assessments as opposed to his friends who constantly failed. He flicked through the book and found the word 'Pre-destination' in bold print. The definition for the word said: 'The belief that everything that happens in this world has already been planned and decided by God or any other deity. This is rejected by many theists based on the argument that God gave humans freewill'. Discontented with the book, Remel started to think about King Keys, the man with the black iron mask. All the memories that had rushed through him provided him with no answers. King Keys, The Perpetually Pensive Poet was hiding all of them, but he wasn't present, and Remel was starting to think that King Keys' presence was an illusion as a result of a strong punch to the head.

"Remel! Come down! You're always in your room, come and eat," Remel's mother shouted imperatively.

Remel put his Bible and his philosophy book back in the shelf before running downstairs for dinner. It was only when he was in the kitchen, that he realised that it was night. He ate dinner with his mother at the table and spoke to her about his day. He told her he was with his friends, and they had a splendid time apart from a run-in with another group of boys, but a man came and stopped them before anything could happen. He didn't go into any details but just the skeleton of the story made his mum pause. The topic of Remel's dad lingered over the awkward silence in the room until he got up, cleared his plate, went to bath and brushed his teeth. He was like a robot. His mind was blank, and he tried to keep it that way so that the thought of King Keys couldn't cloud his mind with questions. He was coming out of the bathroom when his mum bumped into him abruptly. She was fiddling with some letters in her hands.

"I forgot to tell you... uh... if I could find it. Oh yes. Here it is. Your university sent in a letter. You've been chosen to take part in an event. Some sort of activism thing."

She fumbled her words just as she did with her hands. Eventually, she handed her son the letter.

Remel analysed the letter without reading the words. The paper was plain, unembellished. A white folded piece of paper lay calmly in his hands addressed to the parent/carer of Remel Brathwaite. However, neither Remel nor his mother were fooled by the letter's appearance. This letter, although they were unsure how, had great magnitude, and it would affect their lives in the near future.

"Some opportunities come for a reason," Ms Brathwaite whispered, and with that Remel went to his room.

He closed the door shut, and he started to read the letter.

'Dear Parent/Carer of Remel Brathwaite,

Upon appointment to the Cembling University, your child was told he was given the opportunity to do something special. It is in fact the phrase 'Opportunity-giving and good life living' which represents our university and drives us to do good in the world and the society around us. For this reason, it was definitely our pleasure to make a partnership with the 'Change Maker Trust' for their annual 'Change Making Event'. The 'Change Makers' have simply done what their name says. They have been a charity for those in need, a shoulder to cry on for those who are alone and counsellors for the depressed.

Every student starting this university next year was labelled as an option for this year's student speaker. The information you gave this school upon admission was thoroughly inspected as we looked for someone who we believed would not only represent our university but represent a symbol of change. Your child was chosen. We will not force your child to take up the offer, but we would highly appreciate it. The decision is yours.

If you do decide to take us up on the offer, we would like you to arrive at the poet's room on October 29th at 11:00am.

Yours faithfully,

William Dulman
Principal of Cembling University'

"Who is this man?" muttered Remel as he understood exactly the significance of the location: '*the poet's room*'.

This was somehow King Keys' bidding (whoever King Keys was) so Remel knew without thinking hard that he would have had to take the university up on their offer if he wanted answers. When he did think deeply, he was able to find one answer. He knew exactly who King Keys was. King Keys was a white rabbit, and what ensued was a journey to a different world.

Chapter 3

Remel Brathwaite attends Cembling University. The university is failing and will possibly close before Remel's three-year course finishes. He is studying computer science. The date is September 20th.

It was Remel's first day at university, and the sun was blazing hot. Every September was like this in London. The heat wave mimicked the temperature of the Caribbean. Sandals, crop tops and sunglasses came out of the closet for a month before the English weather took a drastic U-turn into arctic frost. Cembling University was uninspiring. The building was modern yet mundane. Remel stood in front of the office, analysing his future university. This was his fault. His expected grades were extremely high, but for him, they were tangible. He was the brightest in his year during his GCSEs and A-Levels, but he let bad company bring him down. Remel Brathwaite was the smartest and most dedicated student, but his intelligence could not be quantified by the 'F's and 'U's he got for his exams, so instead of going to the top universities in the world, he went to a failing university in London. He had been distracted his entire school life by his friends in gangs and used to leave school to smoke marijuana. He regretted it all. He walked in to the university office and filed in some quick administrative forms.

Apart from welcoming speeches, lectures and introductions, Remel remembered nothing about his day. The only message he retained was that 'Cembling University do things differently'. He told his mum about his tedious first day at university, and she laughed. It was a unique laugh that only parents like his did. It wasn't a laugh in response to a joke.

His mother was reprimanding him for his behaviour in the past years and the trouble he put her through but mocking him at the same time. Yes. It was possible to say all of this with a slight chuckle. Remel laughed as well, showing that he fully understood.

By the beginning of October, Remel had settled into university fairly well. He had only made a few friends, but he concentrated during lectures, and he was dedicated to his work. He tried hard to avoid bad company. All of that went down the toilet when he met Jordan. Jordan Jones was a young man also in his first year of university who was studying cinematic and music production. His course was one made by the university. Jordan Jones smelt of pungent marijuana. He was bad news. On the first day of October, Jordan came into school just after smoking some skunk. After leaving the lecture hall, Remel bumped into Jordan accidentally and dropped his books.

"Sorry bro," said Jordan as he stood tall, looked down on Remel and didn't help him pick up his books.

Remel was about to walk past Jordan until Jordan put out a hand for Remel to shake. He shook Jordan's hand firmly.

"My parents are going to Italy in three weeks so I'm having a party. I don't know you, but you seem calm G. Write down your contacts, and I'll send you my address. Everyone's going to be there," Jordan explained out of the blue. His right hand was outstretched with his phone in hand. It was open to notes and several social media names and phone numbers were already written.

Remel wrote in his social media details then spudded Jordan's fist before walking away rapidly. He pondered whether he would actually go to the party or not.

He did.

It was the 27th of October, and Remel had a ton of assignments due on the 29th that he hadn't touched. He was still fully aware of the importance of the date 29th October. The time was 6pm, and Remel was ready to leave to go to the party. Remel told his mum he was going to study at a friend's house. She didn't believe him, but she didn't think her son could get into much trouble, in addition, at the age of 19, parents started to give their children more freedom no matter how strict they were. Before leaving the house, Remel looked in the mirror. His aesthetic was the epitome of cool. His hair was still perfectly styled after the low skin-fade haircut he had three days before. He wore a designer denim jacket with matching carrot-fit jeans, a black top and his favourite sneakers. To ornament the outfit, he wore a small gold chain. Remel checked his phone for the address of the party and made his way there.

Wild bashment music was blasting out of the speakers in Jordan Jones' house. The lights were off so people could barely distinguish each other in the cacophony of grinding bodies.

"Yo bro!" shouted Jordan in Remel's ear whilst greeting Remel, his honoured guest. Jordan shook Remel's left hand whilst offering him a blunt.

In Jordan's right hand was a half-empty bottle of alcohol. Jordan jumped away, shouting in unison with the music. Remel tried hard to recognise the voice of the person who had just greeted him. He realised it was Jordan, the host of the party. Remel took the thick unlit blunt in his hand and smelt it. He instantly had a headache from the pungent smell of the drugs and threw it on the floor: his smoking days were over. The music stopped. The whole house moaned in annoyance. Jordan's voice came through the speakers to announce a short break as if they were at a concert. During the break everyone in the house reverted back to the nomophobic people that made up the younger generation. The screens provided light for everyone to see.

Remel looked around and recognised a few people from the university. There were around a 100 people in the house and more were upstairs in the bedrooms. Unsure of why he had come, Remel roamed around the living room forcing himself to make small talk with people he knew. After escaping unscathed from the unnecessary conversations, he walked past a table where his hand brushed the side of a bowl of pills labelled 'X'. The bowl fell on the floor and caused a mess, but no one saw.

Trap music started playing out of the speakers suddenly and energetically. A girl just shorter than Remel walked up to him. He didn't recognise her. Even in the dark, her make-up managed to glimmer and showcase the most attractive elements of her face. Glitter sparkled on her eyelids just under her faultless eyebrows. She had beautiful chocolate skin and light hazel eyes. Remel fell into her gaze and smiled out of politeness. In return to his greeting, she placed her left hand on his stomach and rose it upwards towards his chest. He felt uneasy. She used her other hand to caress his face and then leant in to kiss him. He tried not to resist in order to not make a scene. Her acrylic nails crept up to the back of his head and tickled his neck. She released and smiled back at Remel seductively whilst biting her lips. Something sparkled in her hand. Remel stood there, unsure of whether he was excited or confused at what had just happened. A group of her friends, who had obviously instigated the kiss, sat gossiping and laughing in the corner of the room. He looked down, about two feet away from him, to where the bowl of pills had dropped. They were all crushed.

A man who looked about two or three years older than Remel looked chemically exhilarated. The man looked down at the mess with a hammer in his hands, which had come from nowhere. A crowd insphered around him whilst the individual distinctive chatter of the crowd had an enormous crescendo. The noise then formed itself into the words 'do it' which were repeatedly shouted in unified approval. Remel joined the audience to see the man at the centre of the crowd dive on the floor and suck the powdered mess into his nostrils like two hoovers.

"Woo-oo-oo!"

The crowd cheered like dogs in approval.

Remel stood in shock at what he had just seen. He was frozen until a camera light shone in his eyes. Remel had to leave. He left the house as quickly as possible. Once he had left the house, he was hit by the cool breeze in contrast to the stuffy environment which had just ensnared him. He took the first bus going to his house. Once he was four stops away, Remel decided to check the time. It was 23:30. He turned the screen of his phone off. When the screen was black, he looked at his reflection. He gasped in shock at the sight. He looked fine, but there was one thing missing: his gold chain. A knife was shoved straight into Remel's mood, killing the sliver of happiness he had left.

Remel got home, had a shower, brushed his teeth and then went to bed like a robot—void of emotion—following a simple routine programmed into him.

Remel had woken up at 7am the next morning after the party to start working on his assignments. He had his laptop next to him, and he typed faster than light speed about computers. His mother came down the stairs. He recognised her footsteps. She was storming.

"Mum, I made breakfast!" Remel shouted.

The door to the living room flung open, and his laptop was yanked out of his grip so quickly it was almost simultaneous. Remel looked at his mother who still looked half asleep. Fury radiated dangerously under the bags under her eyes. With one hand she held Remel's laptop and the other her hand was clenched tightly into a fist. The fist-clenched hand released to reach into her pyjama pockets. She took out her phone, unlocked it and turned it towards Remel. He was watching the video of a wild rave. The rave was taking place in a house where people crowded together to see a man, who looked chemically exhilarated, snort a heap of crushed pills. In the seconds that followed, the camera focussed on the crowd who cheered ecstatically. The camera then caught the glimpse of a boy who looked like he didn't want to be there at all, and his eyes squinted as the flash of the camera shone directly in his face. Remel recognised himself and looked up to his mother with puppy eyes.

"Junior! What is wrong with you? Your father and I raised you better than this. You're in university. You're a man, and you still can't see the effects of your actions. Your father may not be here anymore, but I have tried my best to emulate the example he set. I have tried my best to lead you on the right path. I have supported you financially and emotionally all your life. I work as an accountant not because it's fun, but because I needed to make sure you have everything you need. My job is boring. I have tried all types of parenting styles so that I could be the best mother possible, and all you did was constantly defy my efforts with your unruly behaviour at school and on the streets. Think hard about the places you're going to!"

Ms Brathwaite's speech wasn't just in reaction to the past night. The speech was a raw, unrefined extract of her emotions diluted slightly with tears.

Remel stared at his mother remorsefully, unable to speak. He held back the tears until his mother dropped the laptop on his lap and stormed out of the room. He wiped them quickly before they could travel down his face. He then referred to his usual coping mechanism. He returned to typing at light speed and did so emotionlessly, like a robot. He listened to the local radio.

"Hello! It is news time here at frequency station. We are receiving reports that a young man aged 22 died tragically at a house party last night. Causes of his death are unknown, but people at the party told police that he had taken an accumulation of several different substances last night. A lot of which were hallucinogenic. The young man had a severe nose bleed after snorting the wrong type of chemicals before passing out."

Remel felt sick.

He could no more be the robot. Remel's body sunk in on itself as he carried on typing (but no more at light speed). A few months ago, this would be the perfect moment for Remel to smoke and forget all his problems. He considered it, but he ignored his vices and carried on concentrating on his essay. Besides, he didn't even have any weed or tobacco on him.

Chapter 4

It is October 29th. Traffic is hell, but Remel is determined to reach campus on time. He has a deadline for 11am.

Remel ran into the university campus at 10:30am. There was a long cue of students lining up at the admin office. All of the students, like Remel, were victims affected by the school online submission system which had broken down the previous night. The office managed to cope fairly well with the stress. The line passed quickly, and in 20 minutes, Remel was able to submit his assignments without any further problems. After doing so, he asked the office for directions to the *'poet's room'*. The woman at the office paused. She stood up and went to speak to a man behind her on a computer. Whilst the two receptionists conversed, a singular loud bang, rang in the distance, like a gunshot. Remel looked around. He didn't see anyone injured. The women came back to her desk and gave Remel a piece of paper. The paper was a map of the school with a red arrow on the *'Poet's Room'*. He thanked the woman at the desk and followed the directions on the paper.

Remel stood in front of a dark red door labelled *'The Poet's Room'* in bold italic writing. He walked in. The room was empty barre one man sitting down at a desk wearing an iron mask whilst writing on some lined paper with a melodica next to him. King Keys, The Perpetually Pensive Poet ignored Remel and carried on writing. He was engaged deeply in the words he was writing. It was as if he was transported into another world, completely oblivious to the physical realm he existed in, and as an effect couldn't stop writing. Whatever he was seeing/thinking was flooding on to the paper actively. He *was* pensive. Remel looked around the room. He had never been to this part of the university. It was possibly the oldest and shabbiest building on campus. The desks were old, wooden and Victorian looking. The chairs were exactly the same. Around the class there were old paintbrushes and art equipment accompanied by pencils and used lined pieces of paper which were scattered everywhere. At the back of the room was a light blue door, just as ancient as the room itself, which wasn't closed. The door was opening and closing forcefully due to the strong winds outside. Remel stood awkwardly at the entrance, feeling unable to speak. His focus switched from King Keys and the blue door. Finally, he gained the courage.

"Who are you?"

Remel said, coming off stronger than he was supposed to.

"I am you here onwards. The man in your mirror is me as well. I wonder from here on what type of story I will tell…"

King Keys replied whilst reading the paper he was writing on.

Remel was confused, and he wondered what to say. He looked directly at King Keys, trying to decipher the neutral expression on his mask.

"I'm working in partnership with the 'Change Makers Charity'. They are doing work all over the world with multiple organisations to provide education, healthcare, emotional/mental support, clothes and hope to everyone possible. They do everything. In three months' time, we will be having a festival in central London to bring awareness of our work. We would like you to do a speech from your perspective as a young man living in London of your ideas on the world and what we need to do to change it," continued King Keys without a cryptic answer or any consideration for Remel's discombobulated look.

Remel stared at King Keys. The room was silent. Remel analysed the mysterious figure in front of him and wondered if he was real. In recent times, it had been hard for Remel to cope with his emotions. He had to come to terms with troubling memories and painful aspects of his past. The specific memory of his father's death could have been the possible catalyst of the deterioration of Remel's mental state.

"I'm real. Touch my hand," the masked man said, provoking Remel.

The mood of the room changed. His confusion grew malignantly. Remel was filled with a fiery and shocking burst of adrenaline. His heart pounded rapidly. He lunged at King Keys over the table grabbing the collar of his shirt so tightly that he was gasping for air. Remel couldn't let go. He tensed both his hands and gripped onto his neck like two pigeons attacking their food in vicious hunger. His face went red, dissimilar to other people of his complexion. Remel disregarded the fact that his body was flat on the table, because his hands were all he needed for his spontaneous attack. King Keys was on track to being asphyxiated, and his mask shook like a life sized bobble-head, unable to control itself. The mask was coming loose. Then suddenly, Remel became weak. Every muscle in his body lost its strength and he crumbled on the table. His arms and legs fell powerlessly, and his torso held the weight of all his body whilst his arms and legs dangled off of the table and drooped on to the floor. King Keys fixed his mask and shirt then stood up.

"I have special abilities," King Keys explained before releasing Remel from his weakening mental hold.

Remel regained control of his body and slid off of the table onto his two feet. He was lost for words. He tried to find a way to wake up after King Keys had just confirmed what he was: a character from his nightmares. Remel stood tall and resumed the staring contest that had started since he had walked into the room. He had a sickening feeling in his belly. A possible sign from his body to say that he wasn't dreaming and that this was reality whether or not he was prepared for it. King Keys looked deep into Remel's eyes and grasped his sense of fear. It was a nauseating fear that reverted Remel's soul into that of an infant. Remel tried his hardest to be the robot; he tried his hardest to repress his emotion and he tried as much he could to keep his face void of emotion. He tried in vain. Remel was as scared as a toddler looking at his worst nightmares through a virtual reality headset. He was sure that if he wasn't in a dream, he was under the influence of psychedelic drugs that he couldn't remember taking in his drug riddled state.

"The Daoist philosopher, Zhuangzi, after a dream about being a butterfly asked:

'Am I a man who'd dreamt he was a butterfly or a butterfly dreaming he was a man?'" explained Keys in response to Remel's thoughts before continuing by saying:

"Descartes once said, 'I am, I exist—that is certain. But for how long? For as long as I am thinking. For it could be that were I totally to cease from thinking, I should totally cease to exist.'

"I love the fact that Descartes acknowledges that thinking or self-consciousness as a whole is responsible for our being. However, I think Descartes was wrong in the opening by saying that he is certain that he exists. Nobody is certain that they exist. What makes Zhuangzi's statement so amazing is that he starts to question the condition of his existence.

"You are possibly right. This may not be happening. This may not be reality, but it is not a dream. I am either a masked telepath or I am not real. If I am not real, you are not real and neither of us have existed or do exist. The pain stops when you make your decision. It is your ultimatum."

Just as Keys finished speaking, Remel's brain felt as if it were about to explode. He held onto his head with both hands as tightly as possible in an attempt to hold onto his sanity. He fell to the floor and looked up at King Keys with his eyes screaming for mercy. Keys could do nothing. It was not his bidding. Remel just had the option of either believing in the moment he was living in and that his life had purpose or to believe that everything he was living was false and life itself was a waste of time (which was a nihilistic opinion). Keys wasn't tasked with telling Remel which choice was the right one. It was questionable whether Keys even knew which path to follow. He waited. Even in his state of agony, one thing that prevailed was Remel's urge to find answers thus he stood up slowly, suddenly able to fight the pain (but still holding onto his head) and said to Keys:

"This is all real."

And the pain stopped.

Chapter 5

Remel awakes after the 29th with a severe hangover.

Remel woke up feeling as if he had drunk seven bottles of alcohol at once. He still had the remnants of a headache. His body felt ineffective as he tried to get out of bed. Remel's mother walked into his room. She came in on a positive note: not expecting to shout or be miserable. She was just coming in to greet her son before work, but she saw a can of beer at his bedside. She didn't shout because her son was old enough to be drinking; but she looked at the state of her son, who was unable to get out of bed, wondering how to bring him off of his self-destructive path. She closed the door behind her, leaving all negative thoughts in Remel's room.

Mentally, Remel didn't feel hungover but his body told him otherwise. His phone started ringing at maximum volume. It was deafening. He picked up his phone to turn off the alarm, but the light attacked his eyes. He squinted and waited for his vision to clear. When it did, he turned off the alarm and saw the time was 11:30. He had a lecture at 13:00. He tried to move quickly, but his body was sluggish. When he came out of bed, he stepped on the can of beer with absolutely no clue as to how it got there. He threw it in the bin and went downstairs to eat a full English breakfast before having a shower.

It was 12:16 when Remel was ready to leave the house. He caught the first bus that came with complete certainty he would be on time to his lecture. The bus was empty. He went straight to the upper deck and took his place at a window seat. It was starting to get colder this time of year. Droplets of sleet dappled the air. Remel admired the scenery of the concrete landscape he lived in: all the buildings with their arrogant grandeur, standing tall, looking down on the people who worked in them or walked past them, whitened with temporary speckles of frost fading away as soon as they touched anything. The scenery pleased Remel, and it gave him a sense of optimism, although he was unsure what he was optimistic about. His happiness faded away like the droplets of white rain as a hooded figure walked onto the bus. The hooded figure stomped up to the upper deck and marched through the aisle whilst taking his hood off. Remel looked at the hooded figure, unaware of the gravity of the situation. The hooded figure was Emmanuel Akinyemi. It took Remel a few seconds to realise this.

Emmanuel grinned.

He was much more muscular than he had been two months ago. He had obviously been to the gym. He towered over Remel who still sat in his seat trying hard to stay peaceful.

"How can *you* have the courage to kiss *my* sister? Are you dumb! Don't ever chat to her!" proclaimed Emmanuel whilst punching Remel in the jaw.

Remel jumped and kicked Emmanuel in the groin with both legs whilst using the chair he was sitting on and the chair in front of him for support. Emmanuel fell flat to the floor as the bus came to a halt at the traffic light. Remel stomped on Emmanuel's head once and was about to do so again until he lost balance and fell as the bus drove on at the green light. Emmanuel regained stability and stomped on Remel's leg repeatedly. Emmanuel wobbled as the bus halted again at the next stop. He and Remel were now both lying on the floor of the upper deck.

"Stop that. I'm going to call the police," said the bus driver through the speaker.

Emmanuel ran down the stairs of the bus and got off. He sprinted down the road before turning into an alleyway. The bus driver got out of the driver's cubicle and came to the top deck. He saw Remel rolling on the floor with pain.

"You're okay. Just a couple bruises. Now get off my bus! No gangs," instructed the bus driver.

Remel obeyed the driver. He did indeed only have a couple of bruises, but the pain was agonising. Emmanuel's footprints had etched burning marks of agony into Remel's legs. Remel eventually got off the bus and had to soldier the rest of the way, limping to university.

Remel didn't bother going to the remaining half-hour of his lecture. Once he made it onto campus, his only focus was *'the poet's room'*. He wanted more answers. He made it to the dark red door the same time as Keys did. It became apparent to Remel that Keys was moving sluggishly, as if he had no strength in his muscles. They had both clearly gone through a lot between the 29th and the 30th. Keys opened the door without saying anything, and both of them walked in. Keys looked slightly dishevelled, but he fixed himself up as soon as he walked in.

"What happened?" asked Remel.

"The body and the mind exist separately," replied Keys cryptically.

Keys' pseudo-philosophical talk sounded like gibberish. Remel didn't even know who Keys was. He looked at him and wondered what on Earth he had gotten himself into.

"I am a musician and a poet. I work with different organisations. A year ago, I came across the 'Change Makers' charity. They astonished me. They are the superheroes of charity work. They do everything. This year the 'Change Makers' are aiming to spread the word of their work with their annual festival which is taking place in November. Each year they choose a 'Young Change Maker' to do a speech at their festival. This year you were chosen as a result of a bond formed between our charity and the university," stated King Keys monotonously without trying to sound as excited as his words indicated. He too was in pain.

"Why me?" asked Remel (who was finally getting some answers).

King Keys shrugged his shoulders. His expression was hard to read underneath the mask. Remel's curiosity was increasingly growing as the conversation carried on. He thought of a number.

"Ten," Keys sighed like an old clown tired of performing his dated party tricks.

"How does it work?" fired Remel with a spark of interest.

"The astral plane is believed by many to be the universe of our souls and our inner beings. The astral plane is the universe of our spirits. Telepathy is not the active reading of minds as depicted in movies and books. When I walk into the world, not only can I hear thoughts, but it is as if I am swimming in an ocean of inter-connected thoughts, senses and memories. I do not read minds directly. Rather, I exist in both the physical realm and the conscious realm which allows telepaths to manipulate minds and resultantly to read them," explained King Keys, The Perpetually Pensive Poet.

Remel nodded. He was satisfied with the conversation, but he was still slightly unsure as to what had happened the previous day. He made his way to the door. King Keys walked behind him and was about to shut the red door behind Remel. Remel turned back just as he was about to leave. He had one more question he had to ask which was:

"What else can you do? I know you're responsible for the gunshot sounds."

King Keys looked down in indication that Remel should do so too. Remel looked at King Keys' black, leather brogues. They were stylish, but that wasn't the main focus. The brogues slowly hovered in the air: leaving about 3 inches between King Keys and the ground.

"Telekinesis—I can move things with my mind and do so at supersonic speeds," answered Keys.

Remel was mesmerised. He stood and stared at King Keys in awe before walking away through the corridor. He heard shouting coming from the 'poet's room' behind him. He shifted his focus back to the room and caught a glimpse of a man wearing a balaclava holding a gun in his hands standing at the blue door. King Keys shut the door behind him. Remel was scared for Keys' life and his own. He ran back to the 'poet's room' and opened the door to see the man with the balaclava on the floor with no gun. Keys stood around 3 metres away from him when he flung his hand up in a 'go away' gesture. The man on the floor did so as he flew away through the blue door unwillingly. Keys did the same to Remel less abruptly and nudged him out of the room telekinetically.

Chapter 6

The poet sits alone in his room thinking pensively.

King Keys, The Perpetually Pensive Poet was tired. He sat alone at his desk shortly after another attempt on his life. It never stopped. They never succeeded. They never could. It wasn't possible. He took a pen and held it in his fist. He stared at a piece of lined paper before being absorbed into another world. He wrote:

'Admittedly, sometimes I write in fear.
It's possible my life could be ended right here.
Voices in my ear,
Calling me to disappear.
Celestial solitude,
My thoughts travel interstellar.
When will we realise that we are both the same,
So he can stop fighting us in vain?'

The poet paused. He analysed what he had just written, and he didn't like it. He folded it and placed it in his pocket. His watch beeped at the time of 14:00. He gathered his things and left his room through the red door. Once he left the university, he looked up to the sky and flew, breaking the sound barrier as usual.

King Keys, The Perpetually Pensive Poet landed in front of a tall building of great importance. He brushed himself off, walked in and spoke to the office workers at the desk. The iron-masked man obviously came here often. The people at their desk were unsurprised by Keys' appearance, and they gave him a pass which had been made in advance for him. Keys didn't need directions as he walked straight into the elevator and got off at the 4th floor. A broad, English man greeted him at the lift. He was dressed smartly in a designer, navy blue suit (labelled with a badge that said Mr Williams), a white shirt and an embroidered navy blue tie. The English man walked towards a meeting room and sat down with King Keys. Both men had mirroring neutral expressions. The English man took two glasses out from a cupboard under his desk and poured whiskey into both cups. The man did this meticulously as if he was a surgeon performing brain surgery. The English man offered Keys a genuine-looking smile and offered him one of the glasses.

Keys' glass was adorned with a light crystal-like powder on the rim of the glass which was almost invisible to see. The masked man analysed the glass carefully before he even thought about touching it.

"Daniel, how many times have you tried to poison me already?"

Keys sighed, pushing the glass to the side.

Daniel, the English man, chuckled in reply and shrugged his shoulders. Keys held a stern expression, moulding the fixed appearance of his mask to convey his emotions. Out of nowhere, some documents flew onto the glass table. Keys kept gazing into Daniel's soul. Daniel Williams wore his glasses, took the documents and read them thoroughly. He already knew exactly the contents of the document. He looked up at Keys once he was finished.

"These kids are bad people. They are the criminals of tomorrow, and I don't want any of them," argued Daniel in response to the detailed document of the closing down of three youth clubs two months before and the reaction from the affected neighbourhood.

Keys shook his head. He didn't like politicians at all, because they never learnt. They were liars and thieves (unlike the kids who attended the youth clubs that he had closed). Daniel looked at Keys, searching for a reason to feel apologetic for his actions. Another separate piece of paper flew onto the table. It was a record of statistics detailing the rise of crime in the area that Daniel Williams was the mayor of. Most of the crimes were done by youngsters under the age of 23. Daniel offered King Keys a puzzled look. Keys laughed in reply. The mayor didn't get it.

"These youth clubs were places where these youngsters would go and have fun. These were places that working parents could leave their kids for the day knowing that their kids were safe. These kids were learning to use their talents. This was a place for: rappers, singers, poets, dancers and producers to show off their talents and sharpen their skills. You only started scratching the surface of what you could do with these youth clubs. You could have had vocational courses for children who had dropped out of school and any other child who wanted to apply. In this document, it says that you closed these youth clubs down because a few boys were caught at one of them with knives—Daniel tried to interrupt but Keys cut him off—but I wonder if you considered investing in metal detectors rather than finding ways to steal services from the community and masquerading your actions as caring for it?" asked King Keys.

Daniel Williams' window opened, untouched. The documents on the desk flew out the window and so did King Keys, The Perpetually Pensive Poet. There were no birds in the sky and no aeroplanes. The sky was an amazing place. There was no other place in the world where one could go to be so free. The sky was ever changing in its colour: shifting between light shades of blue that cried innocence and dismal shades of grey. The sky was a giver. It occasionally offered rays of sunshine and joy to the country, but more often than not it offered neutral shades painted with splodges of opaque clouds in the way of the sun and all its radiance. The nature of the sky was inspiring in the way it controlled the people living their lives underneath it unaware of the pathetic fallacy which was constantly induced by its shifting colours.

King Keys soared through the sky leaving his own cloud behind him caused by breaking the sound barrier. The effect should have shattered his body, but for some reason, it never affected him. The sky was his playground. Now King Keys was in perfect solitude. At these moments when he flew alone, he felt at peace. He flew back to the ground. His overcoat was like a parachute that helped him to land gracefully.

He found himself in the back roads near an academy in East London. The time was 14:10. Keys strolled into the school. A short, bearded man sat at a desk in the office. The man at the desk was quite pleased to see Keys. Upon first glance at Keys' mask, he understood that Keys was the man scheduled to perform for the year 4's, 5's and 6's at 14:15. The man printed Keys a badge to wear and handed it to him with directions to the assembly hall. Keys walked into the assembly hall to be greeted by an audience of 180 primary school children who were ready to see him play his melodica and do magic tricks. They all grinned like Cheshire cats, displaying their mouths which were missing teeth.

The principal came to greet King Keys upon his arrival and did a quick introduction to present King Keys, The Perpetually Pensive Poet to the children. He unclipped his melodica from his back. The kids were amazed at the foreign object that Keys had in his hand. He connected his whistle to it and started to play. He started off with an original piece composed in the style of a neo-soul song. Where the song would have usually ended, Keys started improvising. His hands jumped around the keyboard of the melodica, and the sound was unlike any other. It was as if he didn't run out of breath. The kids loved it. The improvisation ended on a key change which led into a song by Fela Kuti. The song was much livelier. It was obvious that the song was a favourite of Keys. He nodded his head and tapped his feet along to the music. His body was filled with rhythm and groove. It was now that Keys' personality came to life. The man performing now for the kids was unlike the monotonous masked man who spoke to Remel earlier on. He ended the song on a perfect cadence. The kids applauded Keys for his excellent performance. He took a bow before calling a child from the audience to come to the front. A young girl invited herself forward. She was confident, and she didn't let the audience of her peers put any fear in her. This was her moment. Her name was Helmeria. Keys handed Helmeria with a small piece of paper and a pen. He told her to write a number and a country on it. He turned around and told her to show the audience whilst he wasn't looking. She did so.

"Five and Tunisia!" shouted Keys jovially with his back to the audience.

The kids were speechless. They all gasped and tapped each other in utter wonderment. They then erupted into applause. Keys bowed again before nodding at a man at the back of the assembly hall with a laptop connected to the hall speakers. A jazzy piano instrumental started playing. The double bass entered the track. The sound was magnificent as if Esperanza Spalding herself was playing along with Thelonious Monk. Keys improvised over the whole piece. The kids were silenced. They had never seen anything like it. They were used to either listening to pop music on the radio or trap rap on the internet so something so authentically jazzy yet so different and fresh was bewildering to them. The piece was quick, and as it ended, the audience didn't get tired of clapping.

Another jazzy instrumental commenced just after the applause faded. This instrumental however was far different from the last. It started off with a drum solo. The drummer was obviously professional, because she/he played rapidly with multiple fills and time signature changes. The sound was beyond perplexing to the children. Underneath the mask, King Keys laughed at the puzzled faces of the children. A saxophone joined into the instrumental with ad-libs and lots of power. The combination of the saxophone and the drums was like the striking duo of Robert Bruner Jr. and Kamasi Washington. The drummer and the saxophonist settled on a 4/4 time signature and went into the head of their song. Keys joined them. The melodies played by the melodica and the saxophone were mostly a fifth apart, but they intertwined occasionally as they either played the same note or an octave apart. As the head progressed, the melody of the saxophone started to descend in contrast to the ascending melody of the melodica. The chorus started on a jovial note before transposing to the relative minor for two bars and then back into the original major key. After repeating the head, the drummer did a solo. The experience for the audience was only audible, but they could feel the music as if they were live at a concert. The drum solo was made mind-boggling by things like doing fills on the rims and using other percussions like djembes, woodblocks and triangles in the solo. The solo ended, and Keys had a solo on the melodica then returned to the head before the song ended. The kids loved this song the most. This time they didn't only clap but they cheered and stood up in their seats. He had introduced them to something they had never heard before.

Keys' next song was an interactive one. He taught the audience three different basic rhythms. A different one was to be clapped by each year group at the same time. The kids kept time excellently, and they smiled at their newfound clapping abilities. Keys left the assembly hall and left the kids clapping. He went outside the school and a balafon flew at him (he had hidden it outside of the school in advance and brought it back in using his telekinesis). He rushed back into the assembly hall. He sat down on a chair in front of all the kids and played along on the balafon. The kids loved the sound, and they were beyond grateful for the opportunity to be a part of an orchestra of percussion. After five minutes of playing on the balafon, Keys brought out his melodica and started improvising before returning to the balafon. He signalled to the kids to stop clapping, and they did so synchronically. This time Keys clapped for the kids and told them what marvellous musicians they all were. Keys performed another magic trick.

"Everyone think of a number. Add five to your number. Add six to your number. Subtract your number by three. Add ten to your number. Subtract your starting number. Your answer is eighteen," Keys said to the audience whilst taking breaks between each sentence for working out.

There were a few seconds of silence for some of the younger kids to finish working out. A gradual crescendo of chatter occurred. The kids all exclaimed the words 'that was my number!' and gasped in incredulity. There was another round of applause, but this time Keys did not bow. He had done nothing special. The trick was a simple game of arithmetic he had learnt to do at the age of nine. No telepathy had been involved. Keys got ready to play his final number. He nodded at the man at the back on the computer. The backing track was a keyboard instrumental. It sounded very Robert Glasper-esque. The kids sat and stared. They were unimpressed until Keys started playing a simple melody over the instrumental. It was then that the kids realised Keys was playing his own arrangement of their favourite pop song. The song lasted three minutes, and the audience gave Keys his last standing ovation. Keys bowed. The head teacher came up to thank Keys for his performance and ushered the children out of the assembly hall into the playground to meet their parents. Keys played whilst the children were going out. The leaving interlude had a celebratory feeling. He improvised in the key of C major.

The principal summoned Keys to his office in the secondary building of the academy. When they arrived to the office, the principal handed Keys a stack of notes and coins worth £100 in total.

"Here is your payment in cash and not a cheque like you asked. Nine notes and ten coins. Thank you for performing with us. It was truly an amazing performance," the principal thanked Keys with a smile that showed he had obviously enjoyed the performance far more than the kids themselves.

Keys thanked the principal for the payment, but his gaze quickly focussed on a paper on the wall that had been cut from the school magazine. It read 'hip hop club closed after leader gets arrested'. The principal realised what Keys was looking at and sighed.

"Those kids were doing well. I gave them and their rap music a chance, all 60 of them. I knew it was bad news, but as the principal, I have to listen to my academy. It's a shame, isn't it?" asked the principal rhetorically.

Keys turned to the principal.

"It is a shame. All 60 of those young children found a way to sharpen their talents, and the path was taken away from them. I think the problem about the club was the leader who got arrested as opposed to the children. Don't you think?"

The principal nodded in strong approval completely oblivious to the direction of the conversation.

"I think you can revive this hip hop club. These kids need more chances and you can give them the opportunity to perform their raps and play the instrumentals they have produced to the rest of the school. With the mayors and local governments closing all of our youth clubs, we need schools to provide more extra-curricular activities. What you should do is invest in a new leader for these children. Someone with professional experience who knows how to produce, mix, master and rap. You need someone who you can trust with your equipment and someone who has a clean record. Next time you should do a better background check on your staff. If you need new equipment, raise money for it," continued Keys whilst taking two one-pound coins from his payment. He took the nine ten pound notes from the stack that he was paid. He handed the principal ninety-two pounds.

The principal understood that the money was for the school, and he accepted it with a straight face. Keys' speech had challenged his way of running the school, but as a principal people didn't usually come against his decisions apart from the parents of permanently excluded children.

"But you only have £8 left," muttered the principal.

"You have the choice to build or destroy. Choose," Keys replied.

And he left.

Chapter 7

King Keys, The Perpetually Pensive Poet strolls around town.

King Keys didn't like walking. It wasn't the physical aspect of walking that was the problem. The problem was that the noise of people's thoughts poisoned his privacy. The ocean of people's thoughts and troubles burdened him as he swam: it was not what he was used to. He could have constantly flown everywhere, but he chose not to alienate himself from the rest of human kind. Everyone had problems. Their thoughts screamed out stories of vices, betrayal, sadness and requirements. A lot of people however, also had positive thoughts composed of content, joy, exhilaration and friendship.

One set of thoughts stood out to Keys. This did not usually happen. They were the thoughts of a stone cold killer. Keys looked up at a tall building and saw a sniper pointing at him from the balcony. The assassin had a scar on his face from his forehead to the bridge of his nose, and he held a machine gun in his hands with a silencer at the end. Keys laughed. The sniper aimed at him like a thief ready to bear the fruits of his heist. The assassin was used to stealing lives. His finger was ready to pull the trigger. Keys put a fist symbol to the air. The gun flew out of the sniper's hands and into a plastic supermarket bag that was rolling on the streets like tumbleweed. The plastic bag and the gun then flew onto the front door of the nearest police office. The stone cold killer, without the gun, flew elusively away from the ghost that had just taken his weapon. The assassin didn't wear any gloves so the fingerprints were still on the weapon, but Keys wasn't happy or proud of what he had just done. The police inspectors would analyse the weapon, but it would disappear from police custody, and the police would never find the kleptomaniac of lives. He was one of them.

Chapter 8

The time is 18:00. King Keys, The Perpetually Pensive Poet is leading a youth offender's session.

King Keys walked into a shabby ground level building in search of where he was supposed to be. There were no staff at a reception, and there were only teenagers talking in a lounge area. Keys walked through another door whilst the people in the lounge area stared at the masked man with puzzled expressions. When he walked through the second door, he heard loud shouting full of vituperative language. Keys slid into the room and closed the door behind him. It was a large room set out like a class, and people stood and sat in the corners of the room with their phones in hand. Most of the kids were recording the dispute. The argument was between a boy and a girl who was about a year or two younger than him. The girl was named Coreen Akinyemi. She had beautiful chocolate skin and eyes that were a light hazel colour. The boy was Rasharn White.

"I beg you, please stop talking, because if I call my brother on, you you'll be acting different. Fix up!"

Coreen shouted.

"Your brother? The one who I smacked up? Funny," Rasharn laughed.

The Akinyemi family were extremely close. They always stood by each other, and they would never let a single member be disdained. Coreen's blood boiled with venomous anger. She started screaming. Rasharn's words mustered her fury. She held her Swiss army knife discretely in her jacket pocket.

"Are you stupid? I'll stab you myself!"

Coreen exclaimed as she lunged towards Rasharn with her fist still in her pocket ready to strike.

A woman who worked with the youth offender's leadership team, named Sandra, stood in Coreen's way. She tried to calm her down and seclude her from the small crowd of people who had been on their phones, gathering around her. Rasharn laughed and stuck his middle finger at Coreen. She was too far away to act now, thus she let go of her knife but continued to scream and throw her hands up as if they could somehow hurt him from the distance. The woman had led her to the corner of the room, carefully ducking and dodging so that Coreen's fists did not catch her face. An off-duty police officer with a scar from his forehead to the bridge of his nose (who worked part-time at the youth offender's college) was watching Coreen with a firm grip on his concealed gun. The officer was called PC Connor. He was ready to intervene, but Sandra had everything under control. Keys walked to the middle of the crowd of young people. They all jumped and shouted as if they were at a rave. The officer was disgusted by Keys' presence.

"Settle down. Sit in your seats," Keys commanded.

All the kids listened to him and made their way to their seats. The woman who was calming down Coreen in the corner turned around to see the man who had set order to the chaos of her session. Rasharn White sat silently as he listened to the mysterious man who had saved him and his friends from tragedy two months prior. Sandra recognised the man in the mask and gave him thumbs up before returning to Coreen (who was less agitated than before).

"This is a safe environment for all of you. This is a place where no one is allowed to judge you for your past. This is a place where you are who you are and you become what you want to be. Sandra over here—he said whilst pointing at the woman speaking to Coreen—tells me that you are all talented people. I believe that you all have the potential to be talented, but I am not going to take Sandra at her word. In fact from what you have displayed of your behaviour, I believe she may even be lying. I want all of you to prove her right. I am giving all of you half an hour to create an original piece of art according to your talents," Keys explained.

He clapped his hands enthusiastically and pointed at a young man at random. The young man was taken aback by the sudden action.

"What is your name? What is your talent? And who do you want to be?"

Keys asked forcefully.

The young man grinned.

"I'm Charles. I can draw, and I want to be an artist."

Keys made his way to the back of the room to pick up some painting supplies from the cupboard. Coreen and Sandra were both facing Keys from the back of the room as his entrance to the session melted away any sense of agitation or anger. All the kids tried hard not to ask Keys why he was wearing a mask. Keys took some various painting equipment and an A3 sheet of paper to Charles' desk.

"Draw anything you want. Can all the other artists in this class please come to this area over here if they would like to share the equipment given?" King Keys said.

A young woman made her way next to Charles and Keys handed her another A3 piece of paper. As soon as they had their equipment, they started painting like fools. They took their brushes and started attacking their papers like wolverines with a flurry of colours. Keys clapped again enthusiastically and pointed at Rasharn White. He didn't need to ask any questions: Rasharn understood what Keys was asking.

"I don't know," he responded.

He said it without confidence and without any care. The class stayed silent apart from the sound of paintbrushes dancing gracefully on paper.

"Write me a dramatic monologue about your life. It could be a rap, a poem or a speech. I expect no less than a masterpiece," Keys stated simply whilst handing Rasharn with paper and a pen.

Rasharn understood what Keys was saying, but he doubted his own ability. Nevertheless, he tried. Coreen took a seat at the back of the class. Keys gradually went through the whole class, motivating them to use their talents, resulting in the emergence of a wave of creativity.

Once they had all started to work hard, Keys connected his laptop to the class speakers and played some ambient music. The slow and almost distant sound of the piano in the piece of music being played took over the room and flooded it with the perfect sounds to concentrate to. Each student felt completely and utterly at peace as they worked.

A man named Jacque walked into the class. He was a short Congolese man, but he had been westernised. He was a member of staff and an ex-youth offender himself. He was impressed to see the kids that he worked with, who he knew to be some of the unruliest of people, working and focussing on creative tasks. Thirty minutes passed swiftly, and the students moaned when they found out that their time was over. Keys first asked Charles and Diletta, the second artist in the class, to present their artworks. Both were unfinished, but they were both incredibly impressive. Charles' piece of art was a hazy self-portrait drawn in an impressionist style. In the picture, he was smoking a blunt. Charles' friends were in the background of the painting, and one of his friends resembled the features of Jordan Jones, but the piece was unfinished so it was unclear. Diletta presented a painting of a woman in an elegant velvet red dress. It was almost photorealist. The painted woman stood confidently with a smirk on her face. There were men in the background wearing ragged clothing and handcuffs, cleaning toilets, and they stared at the woman in admiration. Although it was not finished, it looked perfect due to the outline painted with shades of orangey red. Keys asked the class to applaud the two artists. Another young woman offered to share her talent next. She sang beautifully a song she had written in the 30 minutes that had been given. Her voice had a soulful tone to it like that of Nai Palm from Hiatus Kaiyote.

Keys turned to Rasharn last to read his masterpiece to the class. He had his hood on from the moment he had started writing. He refused to take it off. He had a solemn expression, and he stood up to read. Aesthetically, he looked like the stereotype of criminals that had been pushed forward in the media. His voice was deep and gritty. He read:

'Born with a silver spoon, but I live the life of a twisted individual.

I keep good deeds to a minimal,

I sin, and I'm past feeling remorse.

My voice is coarse from smoke burning through my lungs at every instance.

Flames consume my fate. Salvation feels too distant.

The helpless delinquent:

I'm a nocturnal creature with obsidian eyes.

I've ruined lives and birthed nightmares.

Like Columbus, I'm territorial.

No care as to who was where first,

If I've arrived, I've colonised,

Spread misery and deprived all chances of hope.

I live a violent life. People have begged me for mercy:

I've never compromised.

I've heard God is great, but honestly, I'm scared.

This is my moment.

Death comes quick to the sinner.

I've heard God is forgiving, but I doubt he'll grant my atonement.'

The class stayed quiet for a few moments. Jacque stared at Rasharn open mouthed. He walked up to him and shook his hand.

"Good work, Rasharn. That is the stuff I like to see from you."

Starting with King Keys, the whole class applauded Rasharn. Even Coreen who had sat in her seat the entire lesson—like a bomb ready to explode—was diffused by the dark honesty of Rasharn's words. She clapped quietly. A buzzer went. The class started to pack their stuff and make their way home. Jacque made an announcement to the class that Keys would be returning to lead their creative skills lesson in seven days. As the students left the class, they started to realise the absurdity of their session: a masked man walked into their class and gave instructions that they all followed without fuss. Sandra who stood in the corner and watched the whole session was dumbfounded that her most horrible student, Rasharn White, had talent. He was the last student to leave the room. As he left, he shook King Keys' hand firmly and thanked him. Even King Keys, the telepath, was unsure whether Rasharn was appreciative of the opportunity he was given in lesson or appreciative of his intervention in the fight that had happened two months before.

Chapter 9

Remel is going to the local shop around 19:30. He crosses the path of the students who have just left the youth offender's session.

Remel did not want to see anyone. It was the night before Halloween, and during that time in his area, the delinquent children started becoming wilder than usual. They roamed the streets at night preparing for the moment when they would stand in the middle of the road, set fireworks everywhere they could; egg houses; and play pranks on innocent civilians. No one was safe. Remel wore his hood and kept his head down whilst going to the shop. Whilst he was making his way there, he saw his friend Rasharn White walking in circles near the bus stop like a black cat. He stood in front of an abnormally designed bin with brush like hairs at its mouth. Remel tried to make out the writing on it, but Rasharn stood in the way. He looked up and saw his friend, Remel. They spudded each other's fists and started speaking about how they hadn't seen each other in ages. It was like an elderly person's reunion.

Around 50 yards away, Remel spotted the girl who had kissed him at the party. She was waiting for someone. He thought about speaking to her, but his senses warned him that it was a conversation that would end horrifically. He wasn't sure why he was immediately so adverse to the idea, but he listened to his gut feeling. He looked away and averted his attention back onto Rasharn. Rasharn started talking about a party he was hosting on the night of the 31st. He was renting out an apartment, and everyone was going to be there. Remel considered it, but the girl, who was still standing in the distance, reminded him of the terrible events that had occurred at the last party he went to. Remel refused the offer.

Someone drove up in an old banger and parked near Coreen on double yellow lines. The person, who turned out to be Emmanuel Akinyemi, pulled his window down to speak to Coreen, who Remel soon discovered was Emmanuel's younger sister. They spoke for a moment before Emmanuel jumped out of his car and started walking towards Rasharn and Remel. They only realised that it was Emmanuel when he was around ten yards away. Rasharn turned back to the abnormally shaped bin. It was now that Remel could see it was a knife bin. The mouth of the bin was half-full with Rasharn's machete. Rasharn grabbed the handle of his machete, which stuck out of the mouth of the knife bin and extracted it. Emmanuel remembered the large blade which had almost been the literal bane of his existence but chose not to recoil fearfully. He pulled a switchblade out of his trousers. Coreen marched behind her brother towards Remel and Rasharn. Remel was unarmed and unprepared to fight. He didn't even want to get involved. He had to do something. His idea was almost suicidal.

He fly kicked Emmanuel Akinyemi in his stomach. Emmanuel immediately dropped to the floor, and Remel confiscated the switchblade that had dropped from his hands so that he could throw it in the knife bin. Emmanuel groaned on the floor and held his stomach. He tried to soldier on the pain, and he was still ready to fight. Remel begged Rasharn to throw away his knife, but he seized it and threw it in the bin before his friend could respond for himself. Rasharn stared at his friend who had just dashed around the street like a ninja. Emmanuel was on the floor and his sister was making sure he was okay before he could finish his crusade. Rasharn ran home. Remel followed his friend's example.

"Remel! Did you get the milk and flour?" asked Remel's mum as he arrived home.

"No, Mum! They were out of stock," Remel replied, and he went to bed.

Chapter 10

The day is the 31st October. Rasharn White and his twin brother have just committed a murder. The time is 17:45.

Hastings White ran hurriedly but stopped occasionally to urge his brother to stop running so slowly. This is not what Rasharn had expected. An immediate sense of guilt and horror tingled over his burning chest. Once they had run far enough, Rasharn grabbed his twin by the shoulder and spun him around so that they would be face to face with each other. Rasharn was not a murderer. Hastings could see it on his brother's face. Rasharn breathed frantically as his brother stared at him unsympathetically.

"He's dead. There's no way he survived!"

Rasharn exclaimed in shock.

"I know," replied Hastings calmly as he walked on.

Rasharn took a long shower as soon he had arrived home: the stench of death was detestably recognisable all over his body. He remembered the sight of his enemy's beaten corpse as the words: 'I've heard God is great, but I doubt he'll grant my atonement' rang painfully true in his head. Rasharn searched in his mind for a means of retribution. The only answer he could find was to inform the police of him and his brother's sin. It was also imperative for him to cancel the party that he had arranged for the night. There was no reason for him to celebrate. He got dressed and informed his twin of his idea. Hastings punched his brother in the chest jokingly and told him not to be stupid.

Both of the brothers were accustomed to knife usage. As people who lived the type of lives that they did, it was impossible to survive without protection. Rasharn had always been afraid of the capabilities of his knife. Only two people had ever felt the wrath of his discarded blade, and both of them had survived, which ironically pleased him. He wanted all of his enemies to suffer but not to die. So much so that being a contributor to Emmanuel's end clearly weighed on his conscience.

He knew that Hastings would continue to laugh off any of his suggestions so he took out his phone and called the police in his presence. Hastings punched his brother in the throat, stopping the flow of the confessions from his mouth and took him down to the floor with a move that looked like a Muy Thai sweep. Rasharn fell onto the side of his face. Hastings hung up the phone for him.

"We were supposed to just beat him up and leave, but you took his life. Even God won't forgive us," pleaded Rasharn sounding much too soft-hearted for who he was.

Hastings laughed at his twin's gentle and child-like tone of voice and replied by saying:

"Not true. God's grace is unconditional."

He didn't want to hurt his brother, but he could see that his guilt would cost him a life sentence. In order to protect himself from the dangers of imprisonment, he knocked Rasharn out, dragged him into his room and locked the door from the outside.

Hastings left his twin in his room for the next three days. Guilt was unable to penetrate his conscience whereas solitary confinement had provided the optimum conditions for Rasharn's insanity to unravel as he failed to rid himself of his good conscience. Miraculously, his 'back-up' phone was in a box in his room and in perfect condition. When he had found it, he took it immediately and called the police again. Hastings, not being one to truly appreciate the nature of miracles, heard the phone conversation with the police, stormed into his brother's room and confiscated the device. Rasharn had put Hastings at an immediate risk. There was only one solution: one that caused him great pain to even consider, but it had to be done.

Chapter 11

King Keys, The Perpetually Pensive Poet is having a meeting in the poet's room with other members and sponsors of the 'Change Maker's Charity'. It is the day after Halloween.

The *'Poet's Room'* had been tidied up. All the used paper and old painting equipment had either been thrown away or stored in drawers and cupboards. The tables had been arranged into a large rectangular shape. There were 11 people at the table. Two women in their forties sat at one end. They were obviously the most distinguished people at the table. Both of them were Congolese women. The first one Dr Esther Seko PhD was a woman who had spent most of her life in England. She was the founder of this charity and an ex-lawyer. She had the mind of an activist from a young age, because she could never see injustice in the world around her and keep her eyes closed towards it. Throughout her life, gender inequality was a problem she had to face, but she didn't let it distract her from her goals. She rose to be the best in everything she did. She was a symbol of determination.

The second woman sitting next to Esther was the co-founder of the charity. Her name was Dr Regina Mutombo M.B. OBE. Regina had spent all of her life until the age of 16 in Congo. Her parents had moved to England, because they had been fooled by stories that the United Kingdom was an island with roads paved in gold. When Regina—an only child—and her parents came to England, they realised that nothing was as it seemed, and thus they lived the beginning of their English life fighting in a lower class rat race. Regina's parents constantly regretted their decision to leave Congo. They were highly respected in their home country so it was a shock to come to the white man's country to start over. They were all survivors by nature, and they did not let themselves be subjugated by the western way of life. Regina gained recognition from the Queen when she saved the life of a boy who was about to commit suicide, and she gave shelter to a homeless family in the same month. She was also a medical doctor. The other people at the table were all committee members of the festival.

"James and Julie have we sorted the finance issue from last meeting? I know during the last meeting we discussed the payment for Revolución as well. Has that been sorted?" asked Esther.

James and Julie nodded their heads affirmatively.

Regina then asked King Keys for the order of events for the festival. He slid a piece of paper on the table in front of both Esther and Regina.

"Everything is as noted, but the mayor of London confirmed her presence yesterday so we can confirm her slot, and we have yet to get Remel's acceptance to record his speech," King Keys replied.

Regina and Esther both analysed the paper and made some notes in their work diaries. They discussed other miscellaneous subjects. Esther made the summarising point. As all members of the committee started to leave, Remel had just come into the room. He was confused as to what was happening. Regina approached him and shook his hand. She offered him a genuine smile, but he had absolutely no clue as to who she was.

"You must be Mr Brathwaite," stated Regina with confidence and a slight afro-francophone accent.

Remel was extremely on edge at this point. He had never seen this woman in his life. He glanced at King Keys out of the corner of his eye and wondered what exactly the masked man had said about him. Regina perused the expression on Remel's face and realised it showcased perplexity. She apologised.

"It says your name on your book," Regina pointed out.

Remel looked down at his notebook in his hand and laughed. He had been uncharacteristically paranoid. He apologised to Regina, but he was still puzzled as to why she already knew of him.

"I'm excited to hear your speech. I can't wait to hear it," Regina said.

Remel was completely at ease when he realised that Esther had something to do with the 'Change Makers' Charity'. He thanked her for her compliments and shook her hand again. Esther and Regina were the last to leave the room. Once they were alone, Keys started the conversation as opposed to the usual silence and cryptic replies.

"When are you going to finish writing your speech?" he asked.

Remel was going to ask how Keys even knew he had started writing it, but then he remembered that Keys was a telepath. At that moment, he also started to realise the connotations of being a telepath. Remel laughed mentally. Keys was definitely a phantasm and the fact that Remel continued to talk to him enforced a feeling of mental instability. Remel shrugged his shoulders as a reply to Keys' questions.

"I'm not sure what to write. I feel lost with my words when I try," elaborated Remel.

Keys chuckled. Remel's body shivered. The only men Remel knew who wore masks and chuckled to themselves were the antagonists of comic books.

"A man named Femi Koleoso once told me that being lost is a state of mind like a man finding himself in the wilderness and deciding that the wilderness is his home," Keys explained.

Remel was addled. He didn't understand the relevance of the story at that moment so he paid no attention to it. Keys continued speaking.

"You are the one who decides whether you are lost for words or not. Whatever you are feeling at any moment can be conveyed through your speech. As people, we have the ability to harness the power of words. When you feel lost for words, you are confused so speak about your feeling of confusion in the context of what you are saying and relate it to your audience."

Once Keys had finished speaking, Remel understood the meaning of the anecdote. Remel started to leave the 'Poet's Room' without saying goodbye. Keys stopped Remel at the door and congratulated him for his actions on the eve of Halloween. Remel was addled again until he remembered what had happened with Coreen, Rasharn and Emmanuel. He smirked as he left the room, because he realised his actions where those of a superhero, and he vowed to carry on doing good works whenever he could.

Chapter 12

Remel is in his room finishing off his assignments whilst listening to music.

Remel was proud of his work. He had just written a nine-page essay concerning the principles of digital communications. He read over his work thoroughly whilst an old Kanye West album was playing in the background. Once he had finished his essay, he started thinking about his speech. He roamed the internet and searched his philosophy book for inspiration. He couldn't find anything until inspiration came from where he didn't expect. The song that was playing featured Nas. Kanye West's first verse painted multiple images of feeling positive in negative situations and hoping for the best but it was Nas' verse (recognised by some to be his best verse ever) which inspired Remel.

He started off his verse by rapping about being unsure what to rap about. He detailed all his options, for example: guns, religion, money or racial issues. In his opening lines, he essentially depicted the dilemma of every rapper: they can either fit into the stereotype of being a misogynistic and materialistic criminal or they can use their words as a means of activism and discussion of social issues. Remel imagined that Nas had a kind of writer's block when he was writing the song. He almost felt as if he could empathise with the verse apart from the fact that Nas persisted to write in spite of his mental barrier, whereas Remel's speech existed only as a blank piece of paper. He picked up his philosophy book and flicked through it. He landed on a page titled change. At the top of the page, there was a quote in bold lettering from Heraclitus. The quote said, 'One cannot step into the same river twice'. Remel started to think about how he felt after the death of his father; how he felt after reading his GCSE results and realising he had failed himself and his parents (father included); his mother in general and multiple other things that came in and out of his life. He read some other quotes by Zeno, Aristotle and Plato before he started writing a storm.

Remel spotted a small piece of paper on the floor which hadn't been there before. It read: 'Everything you are doing now is useless'. It was obviously a message from King Keys. Remel wasn't sure what the point of the note was, but it reminded him of the idea of nihilism. He scrunched it up and threw it in the bin.

Chapter 13

Remel is on his way to the university to hand in his assignment. The online submission service is down again. The date is the 2nd November.

It was a normal day. Remel had no reason to see King Keys, and there was no one after him. The weather was gradually becoming colder, but it was a problem that was easily solved by extra layers and a coat. Remel arrived at the university an hour before his deadline and handed in his assignment. Once he was on campus, Remel decided to go to the library. The library was filled with students finishing their assignments at the last minute. There were no empty tables so Remel had to join a girl who was sitting down at the closest table to him. She had headphones in and she was deeply engaged in her revision on visual arts. Remel left his belongings at his chair and went to find some revision materials from the bookshelves before making his way back to his seat. He had been in the library for an hour when his mum called him. She had asked him where he was and when he would be coming home. When he replied by saying 'in 30 minutes' and his mother snapped at him, Remel realised something had happened. He hung up the phone, gathered his belongings and left the library immediately. He ordered a taxi from the university and made his way home. A dark silence greeted him at the door. Remel walked straight into the living room and saw Adira sitting with two police officers. She had obviously been crying a river. Her eyes were red. She stared at Remel's face, unsure of what to say. Remel's heart burned. He hated seeing his mother so distraught and miserable. He couldn't take it.

One of the police officers stood up and greeted Remel. He introduced himself as PC Morris.

"Last night a young man named Emmanuel Akinyemi was attacked and brutally killed in the streets. We suspect that a group of boys attempted to steal his car so he fought back. They stabbed Emmanuel and tried to frame his sister. He died almost instantly. We are not yet labelling you a suspect, Mr Brathwaite, but we have reason to believe that you know something about the crime. CCTV captured footage of you in a violent confrontation with Emmanuel and Coreen Akinyemi two nights ago. We understand that you may have been acting as a spontaneous peace maker rather than an accessory to the violence, but we would just like to have as much information as possible," explained the officer.

The other officer who still sat in his seat analysed Remel pensively without blinking. Remel thought about the fight that had been about to happen between Emmanuel, Rasharn, Coreen and himself.

"Rasharn might've been the one to steal Emmanuel's car, but I doubt he was the killer," replied Remel whilst still in deep thought.

The officer was about to ask how Remel came to his conclusion, but he remembered the footage he had seen. Remel had thrown Rasharn's machete in the knife bin. The second officer still scrutinised Remel without blinking and took notes on his comments. The officers carried on their usual questioning (like: Where were you at the time of attack? How did you know Emmanuel? Etc.) before leaving. Both officers kindly left the Brathwaite household. Even as he left the house, the silent officer didn't interrupt his cogitation. He was obviously putting a story together in his head like a mental jigsaw puzzle.

Once they left, Remel and his mother sat alone without speaking. They didn't have the energy to. They both tried to be cold and emotionless, like robots, but it was impossible to ignore someone's death. Adira had so many questions for her son. She had known of his involvement with gangs and dangerous children, but she just suspected him of being a troublemaker and part time vandalist. The police officers had come to burst her bubble. Despite the genuine smiles of the police officers and their promise that Remel Brathwaite wasn't a suspect, they were lying. They came because they believed Remel had been affiliated with the crime. Adira Brathwaite's only precious son was now a suspect in a murder inquiry. She broke down. Remel wanted to comfort her, but he knew that he was the source of her sadness. There were no more tears for her to cry.

"Who killed him?" asked Adira.

Remel couldn't speak. He could only shake his head as a way to say he didn't know the answer. Adira realised her son was telling the truth.

He instinctively stood up and walked outside the door, leaving his mother mid-conversation.

Chapter 14

Remel went to Rasharn White's house. He has a theory about Emmanuel's death.

Remel knocked on the door twice. He rang the doorbell and still he had no reply. A CCTV camera focussed on the White household from across the road. Remel knew that the police would've been watching his movements closely after Emmanuel's death. He considered leaving until someone opened the door. It was a young man around the same age as Remel. The young man had a wild look in his eyes, and he looked violent even without acting so. Remel knew the young man as Hastings White, Rasharn's fraternal twin.

"Rasharn's ill at the moment. I'll tell him you came around," informed Hastings, agitatedly.

Remel wasn't at the house for Rasharn or Hastings in particular. He just wanted information. He looked down at Hastings' trousers and saw some red stains. Hastings saw what Remel was looking at and wiped it quickly. The stain was adamant on being visible.

"It's alright. I just wanted to pass on a message. The police just came to my house and told me Emmanuel is dead," elucidated Remel with a solemn expression.

Hastings was far from surprised. Since Remel came to the door, this was the first time Hastings had shown a hint of emotion. His face almost displayed an expression of content at the news of Emmanuel's death.

"We know. The police just came around an hour ago. Thanks," lied Hastings whilst hastily shutting the door.

Behind Hastings in the corridor a small figure appeared. It was his twin Rasharn. He looked as if he had just been beaten up (which was literally what had just happened). His eye was black, and his body was bruised all over. Rasharn was almost in tears, but it hurt him to cry. He had tried to call out to Remel to help him, but he barely had energy to speak. Hastings grabbed his brother by the hood of his jumper and threw him into the wine cellar. This was the consequence of Rasharn's call to the police from his back up phone.

Remel had gotten nothing from his visit to the White household. It served him right: he was not a detective inspector so it was not his duty to find answers, but he was always instinctively inquisitive. One thing that disturbed him was Hastings' wild aesthetic and his expression of content at Emmanuel's death.

Upon arrival to his home, Remel was called into the living room by Adira. His mother was in a better mood than earlier on. She sat in the living room, reclining on her sofa, listening to a playlist composed of her favourite artists like: Zara McFarlane, Nubiya Garcia and Amy Winehouse. Adira had a great taste in music. She told Remel that she had free time, and she was ready to work on his speech. He read her what he had written. His speech was now almost perfect. His mother loved the way he harnessed the power of his words. After her input, the speech had no problems. She was a perfectionist. Adira asked Remel when his event was. He knew it was in November, but he told her he would ask King Keys for the precise date.

"Who's King Keys?" she inquired.

"He's just a man who works with the charity. He has a room at the university," replied Remel, trying his best to omit the fact that Keys was a telepath who could fly and move things with his mind.

"The name sounds a bit like a facetious locksmith, if you ask me," Adira joked.

Remel laughed. He had never realised the comical aspect of the name King Keys. His laughter was interrupted by a phone call by a '+44' number. The person on the other end of the phone was silent.

Chapter 15

*Coreen Akinyemi, the girl who kissed Remel at Jordan Jones'
party, is mourning the death of her brother, Emmanuel. She
believes herself to be at her mother's holiday home in
Gosport.*

Coreen Akinyemi slept in her bed accompanied by a half-
empty bottle of Hennessey and a sharpened kitchen knife.
Apart from the two inanimate companions, Coreen was alone
in the house. She was spending a few days in her mothers'
holiday home in Gosport. She hadn't suspected anything until
she learnt of her brother's death. A mobile phone screamed
out to Coreen from the corner of the room for her attention
but the depressing emotions that had taken over her couldn't
allow her to feel a need to answer.

Coreen was aware of the fact that the police were coming
to knock down her door and arrest her at any moment. She
believed herself to be responsible for her brother's death.
Over the previous days, she speculated what to do. She grew
into a nocturnal creature developing suicidal thoughts when
she should've been sleeping. When she did sleep, she swam
in a pool of her own tears.

Coreen was afraid of herself. Throughout all of her life,
she was successful at hiding her mental health issues, but
recently, her mind had started to battle itself viciously. At
night times, she had always heard a voice that was by no doubt
her own, but the voice whispered into her ear and asked her
to do vile things. She always ignored the voice. She believed
that she was incapable of fulfilling such horrific and
detestable requests until she woke up one afternoon in a car
park next to her dead brother with a knife in her hand. It was

such a repulsive memory in the mind of such a peaceful person.

It was 7am in the morning when Coreen and Emmanuel got into an argument. It was not any different from a normal family feud apart from the voice in Coreen's head urging her to slit her brother's throat. It was heated whilst it lasted, but they were bound to reconcile. Coreen left the house at 7:10 to start her shift at a fast food restaurant. Emmanuel was supposed to pick her up at 17:30, but he was absent, and Coreen presumed he had waited in the car park. Once she approached the car park, she heard shouting composed of cries of distress and anger. It sounded like a fight between grown men. She turned a corner and witnessed Rasharn White head-butting her brother before he dropped to the floor. Hastings White watched from the side with a glove on his right hand and a machete, identical to Rasharn's disposed one. She screamed and ran into the eye of their conflict. Coreen was strong. Men didn't expect it from women. She attacked Rasharn White with a storm of punches and scratches with her acrylic nails. The kick Coreen delivered to Rasharn's groin denied him the opportunity to fight back.

The familial grudge had disappeared. Emmanuel could barely see his sister through the translucent layer of blood covering his eyes. Coreen fell to her knees next to him and rushed to his first aid. Hastings stepped in and booted Coreen's head onto the floor before she could play the role of medic. She passed out automatically. Hastings sunk his knife into Emmanuel's abdomen, dragged Coreen's body next to her brother's and put the knife in her hand. Hastings woke his brother, and they both vanished.

It was a haunting memory of Coreen's. As far as she knew, she had lost the mental dominance to fight the voice and succumbed to her evil temptation. The whole world would've turned against her when they learnt of her sin. As soon as she exiled herself to her mother's holiday home, she turned down each blind and closed all the curtains so that she could hide from the rest of the world, but she knew that the time of reckoning was near.

knock *knock* *knock*

The grim reaper had come to collect his payment. Coreen shivered. She had been awaiting his entrance since she had come, but the cold reality that she could be imprisoned for life was spine-chilling. It was her truth even though it was false. It was an inevitable future unfolding only in her mind. She went down the stairs and opened the door. Before she looked at the police officer with the scar on his face, daylight invaded her place of refuge. As far as Coreen knew, it was around midnight. The sunlight hit her with the feeling of being misplaced. She continued to look past the police officer and was surprised to see people of all colours and cultures. Gosport was a predominantly white area, and she hadn't seen any coloured people there before. She had only been in Gosport for two weeks, and it had already changed unrecognisably. A large double-decker bus passed by. The more she analysed her surroundings, the more she realised she was never in Gosport. The area was in fact in London.

How she had gotten from Gosport to London without leaving the house was impossible to fathom. Nostalgia hit her. It had only been two weeks, but she missed London already. She had expected to never be able to see the cohesion and unity of all the world's cultures as she did in her area again. She had cut herself off from the rest of the world (or so she thought), but her sudden teleportation tested her sanity. Before the scarred police officer could greet her, Coreen collapsed and she lay on the floor for a few moments unable to comprehend why God had cursed her with the blessing of coming to her own home.

She was unaware that it was not God's bidding.

Chapter 16

*Derrick Hodge, Robert Dilan, Dennissa Cole, Nikola West, Nate Smith, Lonnie Lynn and Germaine Cole are all in **the office**. Their eighth member is working on the next course of action. The time is 13:45.*

As always, the computer-lit room was filled with an eerie atmosphere and freezing temperatures, but the group persisted to meet despite the non-existent heaters. In the corner of the room, lay a melodica next to Lonnie Lynn, a brooding, Swedish-Somali man, who sat quietly whilst playing with his Rubik's cube as if he was completely oblivious to the discussion between his peers. He was a hacker, a fugitive and criminal but an overall kind gentleman. His past was a dark mystery fuelled by his hatred for the system that he had been stuck in from birth. The first epiphany Lonnie had was after reading the opening excerpt from a book titled 'Honey Theory: The illusion of free will' which read:

'Honey is flower nectar collected by bees which is broken down into simple sugars and stored inside honeycomb. The flavour, texture and colour of honey are dependent on the environment of the bee, because different flowers have different nectars.

Free will is and always has been a myth since the fall of man. It has been programmed into us psychologically to absorb knowledge from our surroundings constantly. To some extent, we live in a time where freedom is even more non-existent than ever because at each second of our lives—even during sleep—we are being bombarded with information from music, TV shows, movies and by communicating with other people. They subliminally convey their experiences to us to a point that we are no more ourselves but a product of the memories of our experiences.

We are just like honey.

Whilst writing this book, there was one troubling fact that I hadn't quite considered: if we (as human beings) are products of information (primarily the media) then those who control the media control us. If this part of my theory is correct then there is truly no hope for individuality or human rights.'

Lonnie's response to the excerpt was radical yet simple: for him to find freedom, he was to take away the power from those who controlled the media. It was a Goliath of a task, which was almost impossible to complete alone.

He was unaware of the irony in his ambition.

For the first five years, Lonnie had been beyond successful in his mission. Somehow, he had been able to uncover secrets of the existence of the clandestine oligarchs who ruled over publishing companies, record labels, journalists and the likes for years. His weapon of choice was usually a laptop which he utilised to hack into endless numbers of databases. However, on one of his most dangerous of missions his only option was to break into the home of a TV mogul who was the key for him to finally complete his greatest work. His aim was to cause a crisis that would practically erupt across all forms of media and would result in the end of the tyranny of 'information'.

Lonnie's break-in was successful. He crept in through an open back door which he had *borrowed* the key to. In the unlit and opaque room, some golden vases and ornamented paintings glimmered. The minute sparkles latched onto Lonnie's attention, but he reminded himself that he was there to steal documents and not valuable possessions. He was aware that the owner of the home was on a date with his ex-girlfriend's sister, but he still crept silently. He found his way up the velvet stairs and into an office on the third floor of the house.

A pair of footsteps flittered in a bedroom across the corridor.

Lonnie fell into the office, grabbed the large envelope from an adjacent shelve, which he had come to take and zipped towards the stairs. The bedroom door opened and out came a muscular man who was dressed only in boxers. The man held a samurai sword in his hand that looked like its primary purpose was to be a piece of art on his wall. Regardless, he was still able to use it as a weapon. *No one was supposed to be here*, thought Lonnie. An almost nude woman stood behind the man and cried:

"Babe! I'm calling the police. Catch him!"

This was not Lonnie's plan. He sped down the stairs at light speed, but the envelope dropped out of his hand halfway. He grabbed it and tried to continue running, but he fell painfully. The boxer-clothed man swung his sword down onto Lonnie's leg. His foot was crushed and his ankle peeped out of his skin. The agonising pain was heard in his cry. The samurai-sword wielder took advantage of the fact that Lonnie was unable to move so he took some ropes from his rooms and tied him to the hand railings. His friend on the phone cried:

"Come quickly please! This man just broke into our house."

The officer who came to collect Lonnie had a scar from his forehead to the bridge of his nose. He looked as if he had been excited to catch Lonnie (which was something Lonnie later learnt was true).

Eight years later, Lonnie Lynn was found guilty of theft, breaking and entering and accused wrongly for an assault. His home was a prison cell. He had utterly failed his mission.

Or so he thought, until the eighth member had gotten him out.

Through the involvement of the eighth member, Lonnie had found another means to complete his mission as part of the 'Uncensored Change'.

"We can't be so laid back and wait for things to happen. There are people out there that are onto us, and they will be ready to wipe us off the face of the Earth once they have the chance. We need to begin this now and get this over with," stressed Nikola West.

Lonnie dropped his Rubik's cube whilst shaking his head vigorously.

"Don't be stupid, Nik. We all want this as much as you do, but precision is key. Rushing into things like that will get us into even deeper chaos. When 8 comes with the boy, we're sending him back. It's our only choice," he commanded.

After Lonnie had spoken, all discussion had ceased, and all members returned to where they had come from.

Chapter 17A

Remel has made his way back to the university. The time is 14:00. Keys is in the poet's room.

Despite the fact that Remel didn't intend to go anywhere in particular, he had inevitably ended up in *'The Poet's Room'*. The door was open slightly, silently inviting Remel in. Keys was standing in the middle of the room, which was empty, with open arms. For the first time, there was a smile on Keys' face. The light bulb which was usually off during the daytime, went supernova on Remel's arrival. He struggled to keep his eyes open as the warmth attacked his face.

"Shift forward," he said to Remel (who was already in the room).

Unsure as to how to react, he could only step forward. His next step, however, was nothing of the ordinary. Before he could land his foot on the floor, he dropped. In the first fraction of the second, Remel assumed that he had just taken a false step, but he struggled to regain footing. His eyes were unable to open, and he zoomed downwards into an invisible abyss. He wailed for help, but there was no one at his disposal. A cold spot fell on Remel's forehead amidst the radiance of the light which still shone on him as he tumbled downwards into nothingness. He could only be mortified during his beyond abnormal descent to death. Within a minute of falling, and a throat aching from screaming, he was able to open his eyes to find himself on a metallic floor completely unlike the one in *'The Poet's Room'*. The cold spot on his forehead materialised itself into a finger as Remel's vision cleared. He lay on his back analysing the foreign surroundings with a group of people staring at him in the dark.

"He's up and running!" shouted Keys as he lifted his finger from Remel's forehead.

The room that they had been transported to was roughly the same size as the poet's room, but this one was filled with state-of-the-art technology and devices. The room was dark, and the little amount of light that came from the computers was absorbed by the black metallic walls. Remel could barely make out an emblem on the wall which read 'Uncensored Change'.

"Send him back. We're not ready!" replied a deep and coarse voice.

And so Remel took the journey he had just fallen into with reversed effect. He found himself on his feet again in the poet's room.

"What was that!" shouted Remel, when he returned to the empty room before fainting abruptly.

Chapter 17B

Remel makes his way back to the university. The time is 14:00.
He is alone in the poet's room.

Remel woke up with his head on a desk in the poet's room. He remembered coming into the university after a mystery call. He was unsure as to why it had bothered him so much, but he guessed King Keys would've had some answers. On his arrival into the poet's room, Remel remembered not finding anyone so he waited at the desk patiently. He must've fallen asleep. King Keys made his way into the door as Remel woke up. His appearance reminded Remel of the absurd dream he had just had.

Keys chuckled at Remel's thoughts.

"Interesting imagination you have there," King Keys joked.

Remel laughed before remembering his reason for coming. He showed Keys his call log and pointed to the mystery call. Keys shook his head vehemently. He claimed to have nothing to do with it. Remel was ready to pack his stuff and leave before his phone started ringing again. This time it was 'no caller ID'.

"Something is happening," sighed Keys.

And so they left the university and made their way to the skies.

Chapter 18

Somewhere in the clouds over London around 15:00.

The feeling was unnatural to Remel. He felt uplifted, both literally and figuratively. He was free. It was a brute fact that he felt in his body as he flew. Nothing stood against him apart from the wind greeting his face. Whilst he was level with the clouds, Remel realised that he had forgotten what happiness was. The sky had helped him to remember. He could touch the heavens. It was an aspiration from his childhood dreams that he gradually believed to be unrealistic. Being five again was amazing, and he didn't want it to end. But it did.

Keys and Remel landed on the floor heavily as gravity ended the fun. Remel looked around to see if anyone was surprised to see a masked man and sidekick fly down from the clouds. No one noticed. Remel assumed that this must have either been due to Keys' abilities or that he had someone working with him to ensure that they didn't alert anyone's attention. Without walking for more than a minute, Remel could see what Keys had brought him to. He was familiar with the area, because it was where he used to come to meet Rasharn. Where the White household should have been, there was a half-burnt house surrounded by fire engines and police cars. Rasharn White lay on a stretcher. He was a chubby boy, but on the stretcher he had been reduced to a skeleton. He had been famished, abused and bruised. Hastings White stood 100 feet away, handcuffed, next to a police van. Miranda and Steven White, the parents of the twins, cried heavily at their family home which was turning into ashes and at the state of their sons.

Remel felt sick at the sight of the destruction unfolding in front of him. It was painful for him to watch. It was painful for anyone to watch, but a crowd still amassed. They always did so. They took out their smartphones and recorded all they could for social media to see. The other parts of the crowd were neighbours coming in the frenzy with the intention of helping the White parents along with the medics, policewomen/men and firewomen/men.

James Cooder was one of the medics at the scene. He was stressed and tired. The NHS had practically been his home for 30 years. During this time, he had seen some gruesome things. There were also occasions when he arrived on scene once the damage was done, and no lives could be saved. The miserable scenery around James supported his decision to quit his job. He had considered it for a long time, but the working conditions and lack of government funding pushed him further towards sending his resignation letter. He had already applied to work a paid position in 'The Change Maker's Charity'. As he helped lift Rasharn's stretcher into the ambulance, he saw a young gentleman arrive alone and stare at the mayhem that was happening. James thought the gentleman looked familiar (like a patient or the family of a patient he had once treated). The gentleman's familiarity distracted James for a second before he carried on his work.

The police handled the situation relatively quickly: Rasharn made his way to the hospital by ambulance; The White parents made their way to a hotel by police car; and Hastings made his way to a prison cell by police van. The crowd disarticulated itself when the fire was put out, and there was nothing left to do, but some people stayed to weep at the tragedy. Others comforted their families.

"What happened?" asked Remel, the inquisitive.

"Hastings killed Emmanuel," started Keys bluntly.

"Rasharn disliked his brother's actions. He couldn't handle the paranoia and threatened to call the police. Hastings beat him up and locked him in his room. Rasharn somehow managed to call the police. When Hastings caught his brother, he locked him in the wine cellar with a box of burning matchsticks and tied him to a carton of petrol. He tried to run away, but his neighbours stopped him when they smelt smoke."

Keys pointed at two tall, muscular, adult twins with identical Rottweilers. They turned to him and waved kindly. He did the same back.

The twins who lived across the road from the Whites were in their thirties, and they both stood straight in identical stances staring at the scene of chaos which had now calmed down. Hastings had no chance of running away.

Remel shivered whilst he wondered what would've happened if he still had been close friends with Rasharn. He searched for words to encompass his sadness or pity, but in truth, he felt none of the two. The only victims were the White parents who had lost their home after coming off a two-week cruise holiday. The path of gang member/affiliate was a destructive one. Hastings, Rasharn and Emmanuel had done all they could to become the most evil and notorious possible. They had searched for their own demise. Remel's thoughts were screaming out of his head. The noise gave the poet a headache.

"Can't you empathise with them? All of these young men haven't had easy lives. They've gone through difficulties that would be hard to bare for anyone. The problem is that they haven't had any support to help them cope with what they've gone through. The only help they've received is from those who have set them on this path. Maybe if there were governmental schemes or family members who had been there to help these young men, all of this wouldn't have happened," Keys argued.

He wasn't lying. Remel could see it, but he was firm on his stances. He rarely changed his mind.

"There are people who have been in the same position and have made the best of their lives. There's no excuse," Remel replied with an attitude that showed that he had almost been offended by Keys' contrasting point of view.

Keys almost agreed with Remel's argument, but he had to try not to laugh at the irony of Remel, someone who was recently amidst their conflict, being so firm in his condemnation.

"I have something else for you to see," stated Keys, quickly changing subject before flying back into the clouds.

Remel learnt rapidly to savour the moments he spent in the sky. He was sure that he was dreaming, but he had no care. It was a vivid illusion utilising every single one of his senses. He started to cry tears of joy. The reason for his doing so was vague until the memory of his superhero father appeared in his mind. Remel once believed his father could fly and that he saved lives on a daily basis. In Remel's mind, his father was invincible. When he was a child watching his father die, he wasn't just watching his father: it was the end of the greatest comic book arc ever. Remel's father, Remel sr. was the most powerful, courageous and loved superhero ever, and he died in front of his son. Remel grew to be cynical of flight without technology or aircraft, but as he soared through the skies, reaching the boundaries of the atmosphere (against all scientific reason), he realised his father may truly have been everything he believed him to be.

Gravity seized Remel and the poet. They landed in Westminster. It was busy as usual with tourists taking selfies next to the Big Ben. Just as they landed, a speck of snow landed on Remel's shoulder preceding a shower of light frost. The people of central London loved the weather. Keys nudged Remel and pointed at Westminster Central Hall. The masked telepath waved his finger from left to right like a painter putting all of his effort into a single line. Remel failed to understand what King Keys was doing until the scenery started changing. The weather stayed the same, but a mass of people started flooding into the central hall. Remel and the telepath followed them in. Once they walked into the hall at ground floor, they walked upstairs to where there was an audience of people, some seated and some standing, watching a young, sharply dressed gentleman speak. The young man spoke with anger and passion. The young man was Remel. This was not the speech he had written. He turned to King Keys to ask him what was happening.

"This is a shared illusion. You are also feeding it. That is why you can hear your speech. I however cannot hear it. I just see a young man moving his mouth with no sound. So the answer to your question is I don't know."

Remel's interest in his doppelgänger diminished just as the illusion did and was replaced by a hazy sense of uncertainty and confusion. Westminster returned to its usual identity as a tourist hotspot, and the duo left Westminster Methodist Central Hall. Remel went home. By tube. Words were inadequate to depict Remel's time in the sky. Time inefficiently attempted to sustain Remel's joy. Alas, flying was like an opium that gave the most exhilarating feeling whilst it lasted but quickly faded.

Chapter 19

Remel arrives home around 17:00 after a long day.

As soon as he arrived home, Remel fell onto his sofa and turned on the TV. The news, which Remel despised with a passion, was on. All sorts of multi-million pound companies presented depressing stories of terrorism, war, illness and failing economies. Remel hated the way the media constantly portrayed different groups of people so that they could subtly create stereotypes of all types of cultures. In spite of himself and his passionate hatred, he left the news on due to post-flight fatigue and an un-rooted, erratically born interest in the woes of the world. The woman on the news looked just like the one who had presented the death of Remel's father: cold and unsympathetic to the news she was presenting.

After ten minutes of short reports on many international tragedies, another woman, with a smile on her face and bright white teeth, introduced her two interviewees: Regina Mutombo and Esther Seko. Remel was dumbfounded by the coverage of the work of the 'Super Charity for All: The Change Makers' Charity'. Esther and Regina started off by telling some personal anecdotes and their cause for creating the charity before announcing the venue and date of their big event. Remel called his mother urgently. She took her time coming down the stairs, and she only made it into the living room to hear the two women talk about their 'young and talented guest speaker: Remel Brathwaite from London'.

"When is it?" asked Adira.

"The 29th November. 27 days from now," replied the young and talented guest speaker of the 'Change Maker's Event'.

Remel had an excellent tailor from the Ivory Coast who made clothes for him on special occasions. Adira was on the phone to him as soon as his line was free. She sent him a white and black floral fabric and aurally designed a slim fit grandad collar shirt for her son. The tailor had Remel's measurements. The next free day they had, they did some mother-son shopping. Remel chose some tassel loafers and a black, slim fit suit to match before collecting their order from the tailor. Adira saw it as one of her duties to make sure Remel looked stylish 24/7 along with her duty to make sure he had the best education and always had food on his plate.

The Sunday after the shopping spree was spent by Remel locked inside his en suite bedroom for almost a full day. He memorised his speech, recited it in front of the mirror and made a few tweaks. The three-part routine was repeated over 100 times. Remel was an introvert who was in constant need of privacy but knew how to convey ideas for the benefit of the world. It was an ability he had lost as he tried to be someone he wasn't over the years. He was being reintroduced to his intrinsic gift. Another note however flew onto his room's floor to remind him that everything he was doing was a waste of time. Keys' illusion in Westminster had stood as a minor testament to the note, but Remel tried his best to ignore it.

The Monday before the Tuesday bank holiday 29th was split into a repetition of the Sunday before, lectures and a visit to the poet's room. Remel was still trying to evaluate the reality of the third. As soon as Remel walked into the poet's room, he was hit by the sight of bookshelves. The only two titles Remel could make out were: 'Hidden Metaphysics' by Roy Lan and 'Hallucinations vs. Sanity' by Le Kay. The poet was getting ready for something other than the big charity event and acted as if Remel was a bystander, watching him through one-way windows, completely oblivious to his presence.

Keys went to a bag behind his would've-been-and-almost-was-a teacher's desk. He took out a book other than the abundance of literature on his shelves. The book was titled 'Dealing with INFJ's'. He flicked through the pages and put it back in his bag. Keys then brought out another thick book called 'Honey Theory: The Illusion of Freedom'. He did the same to this book, but the second time a paper fell out of the pages. Keys pointed his finger at the paper and lifted it up using telekinesis before handing it to Remel—whom he hadn't previously acknowledged—before going to dust the shelves. Remel read through the paper which served as an ordered plan for the 'Change Maker's Event'. 'Remel's entry' just after 'Mayor of London, Marguerite Garcia, tea and coffee with staff @9:20'. The sight of such an important name listed next to his own was nauseating for him. Substantiality and great significance were two features that attached him to the event after reading the piece of paper. He was grateful for the fact that his mother had gone all out to make sure he looked stylish for the event. It was definitely compulsory for him to be presentable. No one not even King Keys could afford not to do so. He began to ponder...

"Are you going to take your mask off for the event?" asked the inquisitive Remel.

"What mask?" asked and answered the poet simultaneously.

Remel laughed and pointed at the poet's face. Keys was a man of sarcastic humour. To Remel's surprise, Keys placed his palm over his face and grabbed the mask. The inquisitive one caught a glimpse of Keys' nose before he blinked and found himself alone in 'the poet's room' with bookshelves towering over him. The plan was still in Remel's hand, but there was writing that hadn't been there before across the back. It read: 'Curiosity is the murderer of its owner. Wait for your time'. Remel, the inquisitive, was oblivious to the meaning behind the cryptic message, but he chose not to prod further. He escaped Keys' lair.

Chapter 20

The long awaited day of 'The Change Maker's Event' arrives and graces Remel with sickness and little sleep.

The Brathwaite's woke up early the next morning and clothed themselves in their most stylish possessions. Remel was in a terrible state, but he made sure he didn't look as if he was. His heart pounded violently. Remel needed flight, the literal means of escapism from his obligations on the ground, whilst he soared through the stars during the day. He dreamt of doing so. King Keys, the missing component of Remel's need had disappeared. Thus his feet were firmly on the ground. Contrarily, Remel had a reliable means of figurative flight. There was a playlist on his phone consisting of 'David Bowie's Blackstar', 'Lance Skiiiwalker's Introverted Intuition' and 'Vic Mensa's Innanetape' along with some other loose tracks titled: 'Death awaits the lonely rebel'. Remel had his own concealed reason for the odd and rather dark title. There were only a handful of people who knew that the playlist existed (not including Adira). The reason for his secrecy was that all of Remel's friends listened to generic trap and drill music. They saw music that lay outside of their preference as weird and inferior.

'Death awaits the lonely rebel' was a miracle cure to Remel's worries: it worked wonders. He sat in the taxi, but in reality he had gone to a universe of his own where he recited his speech repeatedly in perfect solitude.

"You were the boy that came to that horrible thing in the neighbourhood, aren't you?" asked Dennissa Cole, the taxi driver.

She was an extremely muscular woman with a silk voice that contrasted her appearance. Remel, who had left his private universe to investigate the external noise, recognised the driver as one of the twins who had stopped Hastings from fleeing his arson attempt. Remel nodded but didn't reply verbally to avoid conversation. Adira was in another world herself. Once she had gone into the taxi, she put her headphones on, listened to her favourite Jorja Smith and Laura Mvula songs. She then closed her eyes and took in deep breaths. It was a routine she called musical breathing meditation. Remel called it snoring with headphones on. Remel was, for the first time, grateful for Adira's snoring/meditation because he hadn't informed her about the incident. He chose to not do so for fears that he would have to tell her that he flew to the scene with the masked man who she nicknamed the facetious locksmith.

"It's a shame for the mothers and dads. Don't you think? It's a shame for people like you as well. You are friends with them, weren't you?" the driver recommended relentlessly, in pursuit of conversation, whilst looking back at Remel through her rear-view mirror.

Remel shook his head, at her question and her grammar, cautiously avoiding speech. The tone of her voice and the direction of the conversation seemed well mannered, but Remel, the inquisitive and intuitive, could see the connotations of the question which served as the intention of the driver. He felt as if she had put him in a class of delinquency along with Rasharn and Hastings and all the other supposed trouble making teenage boys in London. Remel shook his head for the third time in the vain hope that the taxi driver would get the message. She didn't. The answer however had surprised her. She was ready to condemn Remel for not advising them away from their destructive nature. Instead she reformulated her response to suit Remel's head-shaking.

"You seem like a smart boy. It's a shame that they didn't have someone like you to speak to them and show them the right things to do."

Remel was tired of hearing the word shame. He was tired of the taxi driver and her useless commentary. She didn't know Remel at all, and she had no reason to engage in conversation with him. Nonetheless, the driver wasn't completely wrong. Remel and Rasharn had been friends since primary school. They knew each other since Remel was a 4 foot, aspiring, human rights activist and Rasharn was a 3 foot 11, under 10's rugby player. Both of them stayed dedicated to their future fields of work: Remel would try to convert everyone he saw into a 'mother-Earth-loving-social-justice-warrior'; Rasharn tackled people spontaneously at all moments. At the young age of 10 when Rasharn learnt that he had a heart condition, his behaviour spiralled out of control. He had never been a model student, but the school's rugby team had given him a reason to focus his attention away from the bad company he had outside of school. All sports were no-go areas after his diagnosis. Remel saw it as a chance to turn Rasharn into an existentialist who found something else to give meaning to his life. The retired rugby player saw Remel's words as a fly buzzing around his ear, planning invasion. He always shook his head at Remel's attempts and continued his life as a dilettante criminal. His activism and Rasharn's delinquency didn't mix. The incompatible attributes of their characters put a strain on their friendship. Remel gave up his dream of arguing with mayors, head teachers and pivotal figures in society so that he could stop being the annoying humanitarian kid. Rasharn's defiance had become a sort of reverse conversion. The 'Change Maker's Event' had given him the chance to become himself again.

Chapter 21

The taxi arrives in front of Westminster Methodist Central Hall at 8:40. Remel wakes his mother up, and they make their way in.

Remel's size 10 tassel loafers touched the street in a stylish fashion. 'The young and talented guest speaker' and his mother were the ones to watch. All eyes were on them as they made their way in. People, regardless of whether they were aware of Remel's importance to the event or not, admired the Brathwaite's as they stepped out of the taxi. The plethora of peoples standing around the entrance was dressed in different styles. There were some men dressed in suits with the finest of ties and tailored shirts to match and women displaying the most elegant of designer dresses and exhibiting the most unique of heels that served as pieces of art in themselves. On the other hand, there were others dressed in smart shirts with jeans and some dressed in hoodies. The attendees of the event dressed according to their roles.

An iron-masked man stood at the centre of Remel's vision and at the centre of the entrance of the church, dressed in a black suede overcoat, which sat perfectly on a light purple shirt embellished with a dark purple floral tie. The iron mask had been recently polished. Even from a few feet away, Remel could almost see his reflection in Keys' mask. Remel left his mother's side and walked urgently to the poet. Keys had been waiting for Remel. There was a sense of alarm conveyed by his body language.

"You still don't see it," Keys hit Remel verbally.

"Look at you. You've never been able to make friends with anyone. You hate speaking to people that have nothing in common with you. You have no idea who I am. You do not know me. Why do you make your way to the room each week without any consequential intentions? You barely go out to meet your friends. You hate company. Who meets flying men in iron masks in real life? You are naturally intuitive and inquisitive, yet in such an alarming situation you choose not to see past the veil and ask the crucial question," Keys interrogated Remel with an energy and level of ferocity that had previously been unseen.

People kindly strolled by as if nothing unusual was occurring. Remel was searching for the words to defend himself in his interrogation. He looked around at the people making their way into the hall, but none of them held eye contact with him. Keys was suspended in his position, towering over Remel, gazing deep into his soul. He waited impatiently for an answer.

"You came to me," muttered Remel without understanding exactly what was coming out of his mouth.

"And now I'm gone," replied Keys whilst placing his index finger on Remel's forehead, at the meeting of his eyebrows, before engaging in a vanishing act.

Keys' words bothered Remel like an unseen wasp stinging his soul. The vanishing poet had been so accurate in his commentary on Remel, but he had been so vague and contradicting in the way he had put his words together. Remel felt confused. Keys wasn't there to elaborate on his cryptic messages. Adira, who was a few seconds behind, caught up to Remel. The worried expression on Remel's face was easily recognisable so Adira patted her son on the back and assured him that everything would be all right. She had not seen the masked man before his disappearance.

Remel and his mother were greeted in the hall on the bottom floor by the staff of the 'Change Maker's Charity'. The hall was full of intellectual men and women in deep— and occasionally braggadocious—conversations regarding their involvement in the work of the charity. The AV team darted around; occasionally disrupting the conversations of the individuals, making sure everyone understood the set-up of the event, how their mics worked and which cameras they should look into. A twenty-something year old young man, just about older than Remel, with acne that gave him a boyish appearance gave Remel an order of events paper. Remel refused the offer and showed the young man, who had a badge with the name Matthew on it, his own order of events paper from King Keys. Matthew was completely taken aback. He paused and stared at Remel's paper unaware of how Remel had gotten hold of the order of events.

"Has anyone seen Leroy Kaylan?" shouted another member of the AV team from the centre of the hall.

All the occupants of the hall averted their attention to the member of the team before shaking their heads and resuming their conversations. Esther and Regina came to greet Remel with their usual affectionate smiles. They were both dressed stunningly. Esther had gone for a fun-but-formal look with a white, off-the-shoulder blouse; a black pencil skirt; and black high heels. Regina went for a more vibrantly colourful look with a green, purple and yellow, flared jumpsuit made from African fabric. She topped off the outfit with bright gold heels. Regina normally had weave on her hair, but she had decided to wear her natural hair, styled into big bold curls on the day of the event. They had started off by asking Remel how he felt and if he was ready for the speech. He replied positively for both questions. They tried to make small talk with him for a few minutes, but it was obvious that he wasn't the type to indulge in conversation so they didn't force the conversation to last. They asked him if he knew where Leroy Kaylan was and left him politely when he said he didn't. As they left, Remel turned to speak to his mother who had seemingly followed the footsteps of the masked poet and vanished suddenly. Remel was alone.

Chapter 22

Adira has gone outside to make an important phone call. She is worried.

"Asa! Thank God you answered. It's happening again. I can see it on his face and in the way he is acting. You're going to need to come and collect him... Yes... At the end of the day... Yes. That would be lovely of you... Oh right... I don't know if it has anything to do with his father... I don't think so. I've got to go. I'll send you our location. Thank you. Oh and there's something else. Where we are at the event... They're looking for Leroy Kaylan... Yes, it does... No. He hasn't realised... I don't know. I'm sure it's just a horrible coincidence, but I just want you to be prepared for anything... Yes. Thank you so much... Bye. Say hello to your new girlfriend for me."

Adira got off the phone with her psychiatrist friend, Asa. She rushed to get back to Remel whom she hoped wasn't feeling lonely, but she also wondered if he would've even realised that she had disappeared: sometimes Remel was in his own world, oblivious to his surroundings. When she got back to the main hall, Remel was alone and unmoved from his position, daydreaming just as she suspected he would be.

"Where were you?" asked Remel, with a look of worry growing on his face, as Adira fell into his line of sight.

"Someone called me. I just had to speak to them quickly," replied Adira, altering the truth.

Adira was concerned about her son. He had been uncharacteristically paranoid in the past weeks, and he had been keeping to himself more than usual. Remel had worked hard on his speech, but it was obvious from the way he had been acting that something else had been preoccupying his attention. Adira presumed in fact that it was not a something but more likely someone that had been preoccupying his attention. Remel was an expert in getting himself mixed in with the wrong groups of people.

When it was time, the AV team and some other members of staff started to call people out in alphabetical order to their positions upstairs. It took a long time to get from the A's to the R's, but Remel's name was eventually called. Adira reluctantly parted ways with her son before the start of the show.

She stayed outside as she waited for things to get going. Not far away from where she was, she saw a young hooded girl with old and (unintentionally) ripped jeans. The girl's homelessness was apparent. She wore depression on her face just as she wore her clothes. It was an easily perceptible feature. *What a coincidence?* Adira thought, as the girl strolled across the road in the direction of a charity event. Adira was ready to approach her and offer her some money. The girl stood in the middle of the road waiting for her collision with an incoming car. She was embracing her death. It was an awful event to see. Adira threw her bag on the floor and leapt down the stairs of the entrance in order to stop the girl from perishing voluntarily. Sadly high heels were not made for such acts thus Adira's shoes broke and twisted her ankle in the process. She fell on the floor and cried not only in pain but also in perturbation that she could have failed at saving a life. She looked up when she knew she shouldn't have. She was expecting to see a flattened corpse in the middle of the road, but instead she saw the girl she was trying to save on the other side of the road, where she had walked from, held by a woman with a fabulous afro and a bass case at her back. It was a special moment. The car that had almost collided with the girl had frozen in the middle of the road. The car and its driver had expected to be involved in a fatal accident. The girl had opened her eyes expecting to see the vast nothingness that she believed existed in the afterlife, but instead she found herself in central London, unharmed.

Ignoring the pain in her foot and the people trying to give her medical aid, Adira ran towards the girl. She was shocked to see the familiar face.

The girl's name was Brenda Clarke, and she was Adira's niece (through her late husband). After his death, she hadn't made contact with her in-laws at all. She created a world for herself where she could mourn the loss of her husband alone for eternity. Brenda Clarke was not dissimilar to Remel. The two were in fact very close when they were younger. Brenda's father had also died when she was young from cancer. Adira was like a second mother to Brenda until her own husband died and she needed time to care for herself. She wondered if Brenda's condition was a result of her own selfishness. She walked away as quickly as possible before Brenda could recognise her. She made her way to the park area near the Big Ben and took a seat as someone came to her first aid.

Adira's gratitude for the anonymous bassist who had saved Brenda's life fuelled the guilt she felt of not being there for her niece. She didn't for a second surmise that her niece's depression and homelessness was a direct result of her own selfishness, but she was fully aware that she could've cared for Brenda and given her a home. Adira pondered what had happened to Brenda for her to be in such a dreadful condition. As far as she was aware, Athena Clarke, Brenda's mother, was in perfect health, and she was financially secure enough to provide her daughter with everything she needed. Dermot, Athena's boyfriend, was also a loving and working man so there was no logical reason for Brenda to be unhappy at home (or so she ignorantly believed). The more she thought about the dismal nature of what had just happened, the more she felt the weight of the responsibility she had forsaken over the years. She looked across the street to see if Brenda would still be there, but it was just wishful thinking on her behalf.

Brenda Clarke and Remel Brathwaite were the closest of cousins. They were practically siblings. Every weekend, before Adira was a widow, Brenda would come over to the Brathwaite household. On Saturdays, they would go to the park to have picnics, and on Sundays, they would go to church and come home to a spontaneously appearing lunch that was fit for a royal family. Brenda and Remel were aware that Remel's parents had woken up early each Sunday to cook lunch before they went to church, but they loved to pretend that it was a persistently occurring culinary miracle. Athena and her husband would come over for dinner to enjoy an even bigger feast before taking Brenda home with them until the next weekend. When her father died, Brenda came over more than weekends. Sometimes she stayed at the Brathwaite household for weeks. Brenda and Remel went to the same primary school so it wasn't a problem. Adira became Athena's sister in the way she helped her and took care of her in every way possible. Remel's father and Athena were already related by blood, but Brenda and Remel had brought them closer together somehow. The death of Athena's husband had caused a lot of emotional stress for the Clarke's and the Brathwaite's, but they all had each other to cope. Athena's husband's death was like an earthquake in the land of the Brathwaite's and the Clarke's with a magnitude that exceeded the measurements of the Richter scale. The collective families were like a building in the aftermath with each member playing their part to stay standing. The kids were fragile, but the adults, especially the women, were the strength of the structure. As long as Dermot and Remel Sr., Remel's father, acted as loving father figures to their children, cooked whenever possible, taught them life skills that they wouldn't have learnt in school and Athena and Adira worked hard, earned as much as they legally could and made sure their children had the best grades at school, the structure could never crumble. The community at Remel Sr.'s church provided external support for the families. Women from the church would cook food for the family and send them flowers with 'thinking of you cards' for moral support. When Remel Sr. died, the structure lost its cornerstone, and the families fell apart as a result. Remel Jr. had lost his superhero.

Adira wondered how he would cope, and she worried so much that she even asked him after school one day how he managed to stay so strong. She didn't expect him to understand the question in his childhood state, but he smiled at her and told her simply that Leroy Kaylan was a great friend so everything was alright. She was more than surprised. She wasn't sure whether she was grateful that Leroy was a great friend to Remel or if she was jealous that someone else had taken her job of therapist and moral supporter of her son. The next day, she went to Remel's class teacher and asked if she could speak to Leroy Kaylan. The teacher didn't know any student who went by that name. She then went to collect Remel, whom she had found in tears. He was crying because Leroy had disappeared, and he didn't know if he would have ever come back. Adira called her friend, Asa immediately and booked Remel for a session in his centre. It broke her heart to refer her son to such an institution, but she saw it as the only choice she could make.

Sitting in one place doing nothing was not a skill Adira was blessed with. In spite of the pain in her ankle (and the guilt burning through her chest), she took a walk around the area. During her stroll, she caught her chance at redemption. Dermot, Athena's boyfriend, was a few yards away. Adira rushed as fast as her body permitted her towards Dermot. She was sure that Dermot would be willing to help and that both families would be in their prime condition as they were before after she helped to sort everything out. The more she approached Dermot however, the more she could feel that things were not to be as positive she hoped. Dermot was drunk. It was obvious from his sluggish movements and yellow skin. Adira ignored the signs. She was too optimistic in that moment to have her bubble burst by the truth.

"Dermot! Have you seen Brenda?" Adira asked as she came near him.

Dermot shrugged his shoulders as if he had never known Adira. His response showed that he didn't care for her or her question, and he was too drunk to search for words. He walked around in circles aimlessly, polluting the air with the odour of beer and urine. Adira grabbed onto the shoulder of Dermot's shirt, which looked as if it hadn't been washed in days and shouted at him so that he could come to reality.

"Dermot! Brenda just tried to commit suicide. She looks like she's been sleeping rough. Is everything okay at home? Is Athena all right?"

Adira waited for reality to hit Dermot. She waited for him to showcase a look of dismal shock and emotional pain. She waited for him to be the father that Brenda didn't have. Instead Dermot gave her nothing. He didn't care for her or her news.

"That girl and her mother are good for nothing. They can both kill themselves for all I care. The little pest is lucky to have escaped. They don't give me no respect," replied Dermot drunkenly.

Adira could only gasp at Dermot's attitude. He was a family man as far as she knew. He came into the Clarke family and accepted Athena and her daughter the way they were. He joined their lives and offered them as much love as he could. He was a blessing to the Clarke's, and he never attempted to fill the void left by Athena's husband's death: he accepted it. Dermot's drunken state was sickening. It was impossible for Adira to believe that the man she once knew had undergone such a detestable metamorphosis. Dermot was never close with Adira, but she felt as if he had betrayed her personally. The guilt for not staying in contact with the Clarke's was a knife in Adira's spirit. Dermot's state had twisted this metaphorical knife that caused her pain over the years.

"How could you turn into such a piece of filth?" hissed Adira.

Dermot spat on the floor, narrowly missing Adira's shoe.

"Get away from me, woman," he whispered.

Adira walked away with her head down to avoid the attention of the passers-by who were staring at her. She was like a camel with her head in the sand.

In her optimism, she found an alternative path of redemption. She took her phone and dialled 999.

"I need an ambulance right now! My name is Athena Clarke. I'm at home, and I'm seriously injured. My boyfriend just beat me up and ran away. I think he's coming back soon... I don't have time for your questions! I'm bleeding all over the place! I don't know if I'll make it... My address?"

Adira stopped her theatrics for a second and searched for Athena's address in her phone. She read the address to the person on the other end. As soon as she was sure that the receiver of the call had gotten the address, she hung up and put her phone on aeroplane mode. The fact that she had lied didn't bother Adira one bit. Even if it wasn't the truth, it was literally visible that Dermot had transformed into an abusive drunk. She tried hard not to imagine what state Athena was really in. Adira was put at ease slightly when she imagined the ambulance rushing into the Clarke household and taking Athena out of the prison that was her home.

Chapter 23

Remel has been led upstairs to be seated for the first part of the event. The show starts in five minutes, and the venue is slowly reaching maximum seating capacity.

Those who played roles in the event were seated on the stage. Remel's heart was beating at 1000mph from the sight of the hundreds of people flowing into the church and even into the balcony area. He had felt uncomfortable from a young age in spaces with large amounts of people. The church setting multiplied his discomfort. He hadn't been in a church ever since his childhood, and he thought he could keep it that way. All of them reminded him of nostalgic memories of his father that reminded him of the harsh truth he had learnt from his youth that his hero would never return. He caught sight of his mum sliding into the last available seat. She crept in with a limp and a change of shoes.

Two musicians named Femi and James came onto the stage without orders and started playing music ten minutes before the event started. Remel spotted their names on the order of plan. James, a saxophonist, played soothing arrangements of classic songs and pieces of music by artists ranging from Amy Winehouse to Sadé and even Alice Coltrane, whilst Femi, a drummer armed with timpani mallets and bristle brushes, played softly to give the ultimate feeling of relaxing lounge music. Remel's heartbeat had a gradual rallentando as his heartbeat yearned to match the slow and steady rhythm of the music. Adira caught sight of her son and smiled at him with her thumbs up. At that moment, Remel's fear had disappeared. After five minutes of the calming medley, the duo faded out so perfectly it was hard to realise the music had disappeared, to some. Remel, however, had realised. The music had worked just as effectively as 'Death awaits the lonely rebel'. As soon as the music ended, so did Remel's pseudo-peaceful mood. He looked around and realised that the hundreds of people in attendance at that moment were all going to have their eyes fixated on him as he spoke. He was destined for failure. As Remel contemplated his inevitable embarrassment, a rather large, dark-skinned South African man in a grey suit and a clerical collar made his way to the podium. The site of him unearthed a troubled feeling in Remel: his negative experience as a child gave him an odd phobia of preachers. Everyone became silent and took their seats, including Esther and Regina, who took their seats behind the podium and in front of the section where Remel sat.

"Good morning, Change Makers!" began the preacher with a sincere smile that warmed the heart of the audience.

"Before I introduce myself or why I am here, I would like to thank Femi Koleoso and James Mollison: Our brilliant and fantastic musicians. Just the two of them filled the room with beautiful sounds that brought us all joy. Femi and James: thank you."

The audience clapped for Femi and James before the minister continued.

"I also need to say a big thank you to our previous prime minister for being the one to initiate Tuesday bank holidays. I think all of us here can agree that this may have been the best ideas to ever come out of British politics.

"Now I have noticed from analysing the expression of some of our attendees that there is a little bit of unease. Some of which I assume has been caused by the fact that I am in a clerical collar. I will assure all of you atheists, non-theists, agnostics and members of other faith groups that this event is not an attempt at ambush-style indoctrination. The 'Change Makers' are a charity that does not support any religious group or belief but rather accepts all types of charitable groups regardless of their ideology. Yes, I am a Methodist minister, but my purpose here today is to just be a host and a guide for the day."

The audience clapped, as most audiences did in England, for no apparent reason.

"I do not want to keep you waiting for too long. All of you have orders of today's event under your chairs which you may ignore if you wish to get lost. We have ushers allocated at various points within the building in case you cannot find your way. The next part of today's plan is the workshops. You can make your way to whichever workshop won't bore you. But before we can let you escape, Juliana Connor from the Success through Music Foundation will perform the safety announcement."

Nobody from the audience was quite sure that they had heard him correctly so they sat and waited for clarity. A string-based grime instrumental began to play in the background. His attention was on a young woman, who looked as if she was his age, approaching the centre of the stage with a polite smile on her face. She wore a flowery top, white high-wasted fluid trousers and white trainers. Remel assumed that she was of South American descent from her complexion. Two braids reached from Juliana's forehead into a ponytail. Although he tried not to, Remel could only think of how pretty Juliana looked. She had timed herself perfectly and picked up her microphone just before the drop. The word pretty had lost its purpose as soon as Juliana began rapping fiery lyrics delivered with a level of clarity that could only be rivalled by artists like Skepta or Mike Skinner. 'Pack it up, pack it in/There's bottles at the back/H2O is within' she began whilst pointing to the back of the auditorium. She carried on her comedic rhymes by explaining the route of each fire exit. Before declaring the fact that she herself 'spits fire'. The auditorium laughed at her sense of humour. By the time Juliana had finished her safety announcement rap, the attendees of the event couldn't help but clap almost without end. The applause faded into music being played by Femi and James. They began to play covers of songs that they composed as Ezra Collective—the larger group that they belonged to. Everyone picked up their order of events and made their way to their sessions.

Remel realised he had a message on his phone from his mum saying she was going to the mental health awareness workshop and that he should make sure to actually go to a workshop as opposed to loitering around as he normally would. It would've been easier for her to say it directly, but he just assumed that she had rushed to get seats at the front.

Whilst reading his messages, Remel bumped into a lady next to him. He was about to apologise to her before he realised it was Juliana. They were both of a similar age, and Remel was in a confident mood due to the calming music by the dynamic duo: Femi and James. He smiled at Juliana.

"Sorry I was too busy paying attention to my phone."

She nodded and paid no more attention to him.

"Where can I buy your CD?" he joked.

Juliana looked around, confused, wondering who Remel was talking to. She realised that he was referring to her rapping skills and laughed.

"Seriously though, you're good. Can you give me lessons?" Remel joked.

She replied: "£25 an hour. If you can afford it."

Juliana was not joking, and Remel could indeed not afford it. He didn't however let her know this so he chuckled and said:

"£25 is nothing to me," stated Remel, smelling of immature arrogance.

Juliana burst out laughing. People around glanced at her as she failed to contain herself. She hadn't taken Remel's claim seriously.

"You're a joker," she answered once she was able to catch her breath.

Remel chuckled awkwardly. He felt awkward continuing his effort considering the fact that Juliana couldn't take him seriously so from then onwards, she had taken control of the conversation. Once she had asked Remel's name and realised that he was the guest speaker, she began to show more interest in him.

"You kids coming or not?" asked the woman who was leading the session in the adjacent room to Remel and Juliana's conversation.

Remel read the sign which read: 'Lady Power by Brianna Adiche' and shook his head. Juliana was making her way in until she took a sharp 180-degree turn and grabbed Remel's hand. She scribbled something on it.

"Call me when you finish your session so we can finish our chat," she winked at him and then she walked into the room.

Remel looked at the phone number on his hand, delighted, but it should've been for *him* to get Juliana's number as opposed to the other way around.

Talk about role reversal, he thought to himself and made his way to the closest session that would interest him. A room with a sign saying: 'Ending gang culture by the metropolitan police' grabbed his attention.

Chapter 24

Remel is in a session led by PC Connor: a chief inspector with a scar from his forehead to the bridge of his nose. The time is 12:00.

The officer had begun by explaining that he had been working with young people in 'troubled' neighbourhoods for the past 20 years. He went through slideshows of statistics, concerning knife crime and gun violence that were slightly biased against certain minority groups (who he claimed were unarguably the biggest perpetrators of the crimes) and not exactly true. At the beginning of his fifth slide, PC Connor erupted with vim and vigour.

"Fifteen years ago, I was dealing with some sort of street fight in Blackpool, where I'm from. There were these four blokes who had been quarrelling for hours outside the pub over something stupid. I think it was football or something stupid, as I said, and by the time we got to the scene, these blokes had started becoming proper aggressive, and this guy goes in his duffel bag and pulls out a baseball bat with metal spikes coming through the top, and he starts waving it all over the place. I was trying to stop him, and a metal spike cut open my face. That's how I got this scar here—he said whilst pointing at his face—and ever since that moment, I've been working with stations across the country in our 'vaccination programme'. The idea is to stop all of these issues of pointless violence before it starts just like vaccines prevent diseases before you catch them. Our main course of action at the moment is increasing stop and searches across the count—" PC Connor was cut off by a woman in the front row.

"With all due respect, Officer, I have a lot of trouble with the idea of stop and search, considering the fact that coloured people are much more likely to be stopped and searched because of racial stereotypes on their skin colour. How are you planning to solve this issue?"

A couple of people around the woman started clapping and nodding their heads in agreement. The police officer's expression showed that he hadn't been expecting any questions. Remel didn't like the look of the man, and for some reason, he couldn't believe that the officer's anecdote was real.

"That's a great question, madam. Errm, at the moment, we're still testing the idea across the country. If it is true that this is an issue that is troubling people across the country, then I would be happy to bring it up at our departmental meeting," replied PC Connor.

Remel was disgusted by the officer's response. The phrase 'if it is true that this is an issue…' showed that the officer was truly ignorant to the effects of his 'miracle solution'. As the officer himself had realised that the rest of the attendees of his session didn't like the sound of his response, he toned down the vim and vigour that he had hailed upon for his anecdote and returned to his mundane statistics. Another member of the session interrupted him again.

"With all due respect, Officer, what do crime statistics have to do with a charity event?"

Some members of the session began to chuckle away.

A disgruntled PC Connor replied:

"The aim of this event is to bring all of these ideas to progress our society towards the greater good into one event and branch out more ideas that will hopefully inspire more people to take action. We, the police force, may not be a charity, but our goals are the same as any of the other organisations here like the Great Ormond Street Hospital, Crisis, Macmillan etc. We all just want to make the world a better place. I hope that answers your question."

Remel's phone rang so he left the room to answer it. No Caller ID had returned to speak to him. He made sure the hallway was empty before answering the phone. A deep, coarse voice which almost sounded familiar was on the other end.

"Remel, don't talk. The line might be bugged. We're your friends. At this moment, we're sending you messages telepathically through your friend here. Once this call is over, you'll know what to do when the time comes, and you'll know who we are."

The line cut just as a buzzer went off for a quick break before everybody had to return to the auditorium. The people on the other end of the line had not lied to Remel. His brain was colonised with an army of words which had gathered together into a simple plan. He assumed that his alleged 'friend' was King Keys. At that moment, he remembered that his speech was coming soon. He needed something to take his mind off of the moment which he was still experiencing so he found Juliana and went to the main hall to eat lunch.

Lunch was a feast of sandwiches, scones and cakes with various other snacks like biscuits and crisps. Juliana and Remel sat together on a table where they had hoped to be undisturbed. Adira had seen Remel and waved at him but had chosen not to sit on the same table as them. He wanted to ask her what had happened to her ankle, but it didn't seem to be the right time. She grabbed a scone and a juice before taking a call outside the venue.

Femi Koleoso and James Mollison, the musicians who had played at the beginning of the event were sitting on an adjacent table with TJ Koleoso, Femi's younger brother. Unintentionally, Remel's ears captured each word of their conversation.

"It's all about sowing seeds, man. When I was younger, I would've never been able to even think of putting myself in situations where I would be able to take someone's life. Firstly, it was because I was raised properly and secondly, because there was the seed sown in me from day one. We had aspirations and a good foundation which is what kept us on the right path. We had that seed sown in us from when we were doing Tomorrow's Warriors. That's what these youth are lacking. That's why you can never hear a headline like: 'young tennis player takes a life' because once you have that seed or that ambition, losing out on your opportunities is not an option."

Remel tried hard not to gasp in sudden incredulity and jump out of his seat when he realised that this is the Femi Koleoso that King Keys had referred to when he quoted the phrase: 'being lost is a state of mind like a man finding himself in the wilderness and deciding that the wilderness is his home'. Resultantly, he thought deeply on the fact that there may have truly been sense under Keys' proverbs.

During his moment of eavesdropping, Remel realised that Juliana had been staring at him for the past few seconds. He managed to ask her what she was looking at without sounding like someone who was trying to start a fight.

"The scar on your upper lip. How did you get it?"

Remel had almost laughed at Juliana's question: he was impressed by her perception. His physics teacher had once told him that scars were important because each of them told a story. The tale of Remel's scar was one that he would've left to rot in the cellars of his mind had it not been for Juliana's question. The memory of it was a reminder to Remel that he had been accustomed to the extraordinary before he had ever met King Keys. He was not however about to let anyone in on his mysterious tale.

"Fight gone awry," joked Remel in a secretive tone.

Before Juliana could inquire further, a man in a bomber jacket, fitted baseball cap and jeans made his way to a free seat next to Remel and Juliana. He asked if it was free, and the two of them nodded their head politely as he sat. Juliana began to talk about how much she had loved her previous session. As she spoke, she began to bring out her own beliefs on gender inequality, the idea of hyper-masculinity and female sexualisation. When she asked what Remel had learnt in his session, he shook his head and told her nothing. The man in the bomber jacket tapped Remel and said:

"For the next session, you two should come with me. All these other people aren't really doing sessions for people of your age."

Enticed by his invitation, Remel and Juliana followed the man, who had introduced himself as Stevo, to his session. The two of them took their seats at the front next to Humphrey Anit, an old man who was around 6'4" of Indian descent but had clearly spent most of his life in England. An influx of young adults, a little bit older than Remel, sat on the rows of seats behind them. A woman behind Remel cried the word 'Spartans'. Another followed suit by shouting the name 'Stevo'. Juliana jumped up in her seat and started giggling uncontrollably.

"Oh my Gosh. Remel, this is Stevo the Madman! I didn't even realise," she screamed quietly.

Remel had heard of the man. He was one of those social media personalities. Remel had assumed that the man was present to advertise himself. After introducing himself, his girlfriend and his children, Stevo began to explain that he had just launched his own program to help young people in London to achieve their dreams. Remel tried hard not to yawn. There was a sense of bias that hijacked his perception of the session.

"All of these youth clubs and local projects that have been made to help the community are being closed. We've been looking to the government—the people who are shutting down these clubs and projects—to help us. Each time they reply to our protests, requests and petitions with excuses about financial crisis, and lack of funding. I'm just going to be honest with you people: we are the idiots for asking the people who are causing us trouble for help in the first place. That's why I've been working nonstop, looking out for the community to provide counselling for troubled young people in school, mentoring to provide direction for all the kids who have big ambitions which they aren't sure how to achieve and just to make sure that all these kids aren't getting into trouble on the streets. I'm trying to teach them to be businesswomen and men so they can open restaurants like me or start their own clothing brand like Erin or be the next entrepreneur. We all need to build the next generation…"

A small baby in a white top with the word 'Amaysin' written on it began to giggle quietly. It was as if Juliana began to melt in response to how adorable she thought the social media star's daughter was. The baby watched Juliana's reaction.

Remel was positively impressed by Stevo's vision, but he left halfway through as the nerves crept over his skin. Juliana followed Remel outside to see what was wrong with him. He explained that he was nervous about his speech. She kissed him on the cheek and led him outside to the steps just outside the venue.

"Do your speech right now," she ordered.

Although taken aback, Remel did as he had been asked and began from the quote 'You can never step into the same river twice' to the end of his speech. Juliana gave Remel a miniature ovation as a pre-cursor to the real response he would receive. The buzzer went off so Juliana and Remel made their way in for the real thing. Remel's stomach rumbled with unease. He knew for certain that something odd was about to occur.

Chapter 25

After the break, Remel sits next to Juliana in the auditorium as opposed to his initial seat at the front, ready for his speech.

Juliana could feel Remel's nervous trembling next to her. She turned and asked him if he was all right whilst she watched him fiddling with the piece of paper that he had written his speech on before ripping it to shreds. He nodded his head, but his expression said otherwise. Juliana put her hand on Remel's knee: a calming gesture. She asked him if he was sure. For a second, he felt at peace whilst the whole auditorium quietened. He nodded again, but this time he was almost telling the truth. Juliana's aura had somehow resolved Remel's discord for a superficial moment of comfort.

This was only the calm that came before the storm.

"Here we welcome Remel Brathwaite: Our guest speaker for today. This segment of the day will be recorded live for BBC news," announced Revd. Kungawo Abongile as he handed the stage over to Remel.

No further introductions or acknowledgements were needed. A drop of sweat trickled down Remel's forehead, but he stared into the eye of the camera with an expression that boasted of an arrogance and bravery that he could only dream of really possessing. He began:

"We're living in a war where the soldiers know to fight but don't know what for. Most of us just fight for the glory, gold and glitter whereas a small few can see the bigger picture. We wield a mixture of strong souls and oppressed voices. My choice is to whisper the news: the revolution will not be televised. The solution is in the sound, and our enemies will leave you mesmerised by the lights and the action!"

The audience struggled to understand exactly what Remel was talking about. The trickle of sweat that had appeared before his speech had travelled down his face. The arrogance in his expression began to fade and was replaced by inexplicable anger which he made sure to direct at the camera.

"Statistics have repeatedly shown us that advancements in technology have caused people to lose their social skills to the point where some can barely hold face-to-face conversations with each other. Isn't this terrible? What if I told you that all of this was part of a darker, more serious issue? Phones, tablets, televisions and computers are a means of hypnotism that the big corporations are using to confuse us and influence our way of life for their own selfish gain. You think I sound stupid? Tell that to the politicians who have won their elections by filling your computer screens with targeted ads. Tell that to all the kids who change the way they talk, act, dance or text every month based on the social trends that they see online! Tell that to the celebrities who have been pushed forward to the forefront of the media to promote different ideas that their higher ups are implementing into society."

People began to listen.

"Today we are here to capture all of the ideas and efforts of the organisations who have gathered here today in order to promote the end of all the issues that are ruining our ever-changing world. I am here to say that our cause can only succeed based on what is in fashion and what is not. This is stupid. How will feminists ever be able to fight against sexism and injustice if the concept of feminism is treated as a trend rather than a just cause that should permanently be defended? How will environmental activists ever succeed or be able to take care of the world when those in power use social media to push forward the idea that things like climate change do not exist? How does anything happen if we continue to let these gadgets rule over us?

"My message to you all is to be vigilant. We truly are soldiers, and we're losing a great battle at the moment. The only way for us to win is to begin our revolution. We have to campaign for the issues that we believe in and not what the media decides to promote. We must revolt without ceasing: never stop believing in the cause. Revolución!"

The whole auditorium, especially Adira, rose to applaud Remel's fiery, poignant and eloquent delivery. No one seemed to be bothered by the fact that he had completely ignored his brief. His expression of anger faded. The applause continued for at least two minutes as Revolución made their way onto the stage for a smooth transition into their set. The audience were absolutely clueless to what was coming for them. Amidst all of the diminishing applause, a man named Leroy Kaylan led his procession to the stage followed by a line of approximately 50 kids. He jigged and swayed whilst he played his melodica. The melody was a syncopated and slowed down combination of traditional afro beat and jazz (so out of place for the scenario). It was almost musically perfect, but it sounded as if it was missing the percussion of Tony Allen or another similar musician (which was extremely hard to find). The source of the sound was alien: like the hybrid of a harmonica, accordion and recorder. Helmeria, the young lady behind Mr Kaylan, played a repeating syncopated rhythm on her woodblock. Everyone stopped their noise. They were all mesmerised. Leroy was like a pied piper using music as a mystic tool, leading his audience to quiet and the kids behind him to the stage. A young woman on the stage with a perfect afro, named Nikola West, began playing the most tremendous of bass lines. Adira recognised her immediately. The melodica, the bass, the woodblock and the marching footsteps were perfect for each other. The auditorium was completely unaware of what was happening. Remel stood at the podium and waited for his time to come.

"Sorrow, anger!" cried Lonnie Lynn and Derrick Hodge, two of the members of Revolución, as the drummer, Germaine Cole, came to life, creating the perfect sound that could only have been made by Tony Allen or another similar musician.

"Anger, tears!" cried Dennissa Cole and Robert Dilan, as Nate Smith, equipped with his djembe, shekere and cowbells, began a polyrhythmic onslaught that saturated the atmosphere in the auditorium.

"Sorrow, anger, tears! This is revolution!" cried the eight of them (Derrick Hodge, Robert Dilan, Dennissa Cole, Nikola West, Nate Smith, Lonnie Lynn, Germaine Cole and Leroy Kaylan) together, as the camera woman who had come to record turned her lenses to explore what was going on.

Germaine hit the snare drum three times. The musicians and the children stopped in their tracks.

"Who are you? What do you want!" shouted Remel at the top of his lungs. The line of kids stomped their foot down on the ground in unison.

"I am Helmeria; I want a future," proclaimed Helmeria.

"Je suis Antoine et je veux me retrouver," stated another child.

"Ben adim Baran ve ben gerçeği istiyorum!" cried a third.

Lonnie grabbed his microphone and screamed:

"Anigu waxaan ahay Lonnie oo waxaan rabaa inaan kula dagaalamo ilaa aan ka madax bannaanahay!"

"We are 'Uncensored Change'!" declared the musicians.

At this point, the group had captured the attention of the audience. Most did not understand the mother tongues of the group, but they could feel that their message was urgent. Nate Smith returned to his polyrhythms, and the other musicians followed him again. Lonnie and the kids started chanting the phrase 'acknowledge us!' repeatedly. Within seconds of restarting their music, the musicians mellowed down again. Derrick Hodge began to play a double bass, Robert began to strum his guitar and Nik began to hum soothingly. Their soft playing served as the perfect background music to contrast with Robert's message.

"Hi, I'm Bob," began Robert, still strumming, with his out of place Californian accent.

"I just want to make a few acknowledgements to those who deserve a lot of respect. First of all I want to acknowledge Tyrone Johnson from Croydon who got full marks on every exam of his GCSE's. Your local newspaper doesn't care about your success because you're black. We do not discriminate, and now you have made it onto live TV. Give us a smile!"

The auditorium started to fill with quiet whispers of confusion. Bob continued.

"I just want to thank Selena Whyte from Enfield for her work in providing activities for troubled young girls in her community. Selena, your local government doesn't provide you with funding. We will help you."

Money started to rain above the head of a lady on the second row.

"I just want to thank Catalyn Kaczka from Hackney, who has been helping new immigrants to find jobs for the last 20 years. The home office has said that they will deport you in the next 5 years when your visa expires. Worry no longer. Your new British passport sleeps under your chair."

A Polish lady began to cry tears of joy in the eighth row as she waved a small red book in her hand.

"I just want to thank you, Kerlene Jackson from Hammersmith, you have been trying to close the gender pay gap in your community for the last 15 years! You are a thorn in your local MP's side, but today you have won your battle. Every female in your area has had a pay rise to match the men in their workplaces doing work of equal value."

Another lady on the sixth row back started to cheer.

"There are much more of you to be acknowledged. None of you have been forgotten, I assure you. Go home today, and find your gifts."

At this point in Bob's speech, some of the ushers started to walk up to the stage. The AV team had just received some orders to shut down the sound system, but for some reason, their mixing boards stopped working. Leroy Kaylan looked at each of the ushers who approached the stage, and somehow they all managed to trip over each other's feet. The camerawoman smirked as she caught everything.

A paper flew in front of Remel and onto the podium. He read it as he had been told to.

"The fight must begin with all of those that are not allowing us to make a difference. We are Change Makers! We are beginning our attack."

Adira stared at her son and wondered what he was doing. The audience were now aware that 'Revolución' weren't a regular music act. The whole event had practically been hijacked. All they could do was watch and begin to understand the message that Revolución stood for. Adira stared at her son, wondering when he had the time to prepare for all of this.

The musicians sped up again. They all viciously attacked their instruments in a way that created the most glorious sound. They ceased to play abruptly with an enormous discord. The performance was like a play at the theatre where the whole auditorium had been immersed in the experience. Many questioned whether or not the musicians were acting or being serious.

"Our fight begins with the enemies," explained Bob.

"The fight begins with you: Madam Mayor," shouted Bob as he pointed his finger to the mayor of London, sitting on the balcony, guarded by none other than PC Connor. "You have put more money into your own electoral campaign this year than health care for the handicapped, programmes for young people and housing for those in need. You are our enemy."

The mayor could only keep a straight face whilst the 'Uncensored Change' (or 'Revolución' as they had called themselves for the event) continued their attack.

"The fight begins with Trevor Flemming and Noah Brown who have suspiciously disappeared from the auditorium. Corrupt fools! You are our enemy," proclaimed Dennissa Cole.

"The fight begins with you. Whoever you are. We will come for you as long as you stand in the way of justice. You are our enemy," promulgated Remel.

"Anger!" cried 'Revolución' as they began to play the first song which they had entered with.

All of the musicians had an extraordinary amount of passion which was felt through the sudden crescendo. They gradually reached an unbearable volume until they reached their peak. The lights perished in the auditorium. All speckles of natural light died, and the light bulbs lost their power for a second. It was a moment of disarray. Everyone looked for light. When the lights returned, everything had ended. 'Revolución', all the kids that had accompanied them, all of their instruments and Remel, their speaker had disappeared. The audience erupted into another round of applause at the magical ending whilst the mayor and some other members of the audience sat red-faced and on edge. Juliana and Adira looked from their seats for sight of Remel. He was nowhere to be found at that moment, and there was no one to help him.

There was no need to help him.

Chapter 26

After the tremendous performance, Remel finds himself in the same metal room that he was in during his dream at the poet's room.

Mr Brathwaite was surrounded by the same people who he had just performed with. They towered over his disconcerted body in the darkness of the office. He shot up onto his feet and jumped away from the group as he came to consciousness. His head was pounding. Lonnie could see the disconcertion on Remel's face so he approached him slowly whilst telling him to breathe.

Remel analysed all the computers and technology in the room that he had never seen before. There was a computer in the far corner of the room which flashed with the message: 'Teleportation 8 COMPLETE'. He estimated that altogether: the room would've cost millions, which was ironic because it was almost as if they couldn't afford heaters. The members of the group looked at Remel as he took in his environment.

"Weren't there eight of you?" asked Remel, counting 7 other people with him.

Bob chuckled behind Lonnie.

"You said it yourself, son. The fight has already started. Let's just get you back to where you need to be before you get wrapped up in all this."

Before Remel could blink, he had found himself sitting next to Juliana again. She jumped up out of shock.

"What the hell! Remel? What the hell was that?" exclaimed Juliana, a little too loudly.

Remel shook his head. He had absolutely no idea what had just happened. On the podium where he had just been, stood the mayor, whom he had just taken part in shaming. She looked directly at him as she spoke.

"I want to say a big thank you to Remel Brathwaite and 'Revolución'. As I have publicly explained before, I am of Spanish-Cuban origin so I know that the word 'Revolución' unsurprisingly translates to revolution, and that little magic show of yours was definitely a revolutionary one. I want to invite Remel, 'Revolución' and any other revolutionary attending here today to come and talk to me in the foyer, because it is only with your criticism and your opinions that we can make this city great again."

Remel stood up to go outside and get some fresh air. The previous five minutes had completely ruined him. On his way to the exit, he saw his mother who looked surprised to see him. She asked him where he had been, but he shrugged her off and told her that he would speak to her when everything was done. She went back inside after ending a phone call.

Outside, the air felt refreshing on Remel's frozen skin. He really felt as if he needed to smoke to relieve himself of the confusion that he had just been bombarded with. Reality and fantasy had begun to blur in his mind. It had become impossible for him to tell the difference between the two. His next moment would even further emphasise his confusion.

Just across the street, Remel saw King Keys—returning after his morning disappearance—staring into the barrel of a gun held by PC Connor. The officer was determined to pull the trigger and end the poet's life at that moment. From the session that Remel had with him he had already been able to discern that there was something wrong with him. He lunged across the road as if he had just come out of the barrel of a cannon. He landed heavily on the officer and started punching him in the face repeatedly whilst telling King Keys to run away. The gun fell on the floor and into a plastic bag which had been rolling around like tumbleweed. The officer tried to get up to finish what he had started. He grabbed his assailant by the neck, but Remel pushed his hands away and continued to pound him in the centre of his face. PC Connor left his blood all over Remel's fists.

A police car parked up next to Remel. Two other officers jumped out.

"This guy just tried to shoot that man over there. Look!" Remel explained as he pointed into thin air. King Keys was again nowhere to be found.

PC Connor pushed Remel from him and looked for his gun. One of the officers put Remel into handcuffs and escorted him into their car. They all got in for a quick drive to the station.

Chapter 27

Remel is in a cell.

It was as if it had been the place that had inspired the metal office of the 'Uncensored Change'. The cell was freezing as if it had purposefully cooled itself to make its inhabitants feel uneasy. The concrete floor and the metal walls rejected any idea of a 'home-y feel'. Remel felt fear crawling all over his body. He wasn't sure what he was scared of in particular, but he felt the need to run away. The bars on the cell had assured him for the previous three hours that any thought of escape was a silly one. Adira marched in, accompanied by the officer who had handcuffed Remel. She was beyond tears and words. She was like a robot, rejecting all feelings which came her way.

"You're lucky for all the things your mum has done to get you out of here. If it wasn't for her spirit, you would be facing a serious criminal record."

Remel nodded at the officer and apologised profusely for his actions. His mother allowed him to finish declaring his guilt before she grabbed him by the ear and practically chucked him into the taxi that had been waiting outside for him. He began sobbing as he got in to the taxi.

"I'm sorry," he whispered.

"Don't cry. I know what you're going through, and we're going to solve all your problems today," Adira said.

Remel didn't argue with his mother's cryptic statement. The taxi driver spent an hour driving through London before stopping in front of a building with a plaque which read: 'The Janus Mental Hospital'. Adira handed the driver £40 before they went on their way. Remel knew the area where they had arrived and was certain that this was not their home. The five-storey building towered over him and assured him that the worst was yet to come. He followed his mother into the building. She walked past the front desk and up the stairs to the first floor. She knocked on a door which was labelled 'Dr Damagh's office'. A tall Egyptian/Arabian looking man came through with a wide smile on his face. He hugged Adira before turning his attention to her son.

"Hello, Remel. We've met before when you were younger, but I'm sure you wouldn't remember me now. It must've been close to 15 years ago."

Remel took a seat at a desk with Asa's chair opposite him. Remel slowly began to recognise the man, but his memory was still vague.

The small room was lit only by a lamp next to the laptop. The wooden walls left a vintage feel. On the walls were some pictures of some famous movies. The only one Remel could recognise was The Matrix.

"Your mother has told me recently that you haven't been feeling well. Is that true?" asked Asa.

"No. I'm perfect," replied Remel much to his mother's chagrin.

Asa paused before continuing.

"That's all right. So talk to me about what happened today at the 'Change Maker's Event'."

Asa had chosen his words carefully. Remel also had to pause before answering.

"I don't know," he answered simply.

"Do you know the names of the people you performed with?" questioned Asa as if they were in an interrogation room.

Remel nodded his head. Asa handed him a piece of paper to write their names down. After a few seconds of arguing with himself about whether he should or shouldn't have done so, he began to write. Asa read the names Remel had given to him before typing them on his laptop. He tried to ask Remel a few more questions about, 'Revolución', his father and his life, but Remel wouldn't answer. Once Asa realised that he had simply been attempting to draw blood from a stone, he called his assistant via intercom and told her to bring up his paper from the printer. He walked in the room swiftly with a single A4 sheet and handed it to Remel. He left. The room was void of any sound. Remel looked at the paper and gasped at what he was seeing. Asa perused Remel's expression and began to type things into his laptop again.

"Do you recognise these people?" asked Asa.

Remel nodded his head, but what he was seeing was impossible. The paper in front of him held the images of seven musicians who he enjoyed listening to. The seven of them were identical to a member of 'Revolución', apart from Leroy Kaylan who had no counterpart in the pictures. Two of the musicians, Ghostface Killah and J. Cole, although male looked just like the twins that were at the incident at Rasharn's house. In fact, he realised at that point, with startled surprise, that they were Germaine and Dennissa, two of the musicians he had just performed with. The two rappers looked nothing alike, but somehow their female counterparts had merged enough of the two rappers characteristics to bear uncanny resemblances to each other and their celebrities. Remel turned in his chair to wave the paper in his mother's face frantically. He pointed to one of the rappers and said:

"Don't you remember her? Our taxi driver from this morning! And look: I performed with these people today."

Adira shook her head at her son.

"Remel. Today at the Change Maker's Event, you performed with a backing track. From the information I've been given, you've shown many symptoms recently. We're going to have to keep you here over the next few weeks to see exactly what's wrong and how we can treat you."

Remel had already had his share of prison for the day. He stormed out of the room and ran downstairs to the foyer. Two security guards stood at the entrance. He tried to run past them into the streets, but the first guard stopped Remel whilst the second one got behind him and injected him with a serum of the tranquilising nature. Asa came downstairs and helped to drag Remel into his quarters as if he was an inhabitant of an asylum for the insane. Adira stayed in his office and cried quietly, hoping that she was doing right for her son.

*****

Remel has been in and out of the hospital for 11 months without any diagnosis. Asa is planning to release him permanently within a week. The date is October 29th. The time is 16:00.

Asa and Adira had come to visit Remel in his quarters, holding hands. They opened the door to find Remel on his laptop, lost in an episode of his favourite anime. Over the 11 months Remel had spent in inconsistent isolation, the laptop was one of his only companions. He had lost contact with the little amount of friends that he had left, he had lost contact with the outside world and he had lost contact with the masked man who, during his stay at the hospital, he had been forced to believe was a figment of his imagination. His only friend was Coreen Akinyemi, who he had become friends with, after he found that she too had been admitted to the hospital. A small gold chain was offered by her as a peace offering between them. She wouldn't talk to Remel about why she was admitted so he respected her privacy as she respected his. Eventually, their mutual respect became a foundation for trust. Adira and Asa had also grown closer over the 11 months.

"Remel, this is all going to be over soon. You can come back home by next week," Adira spoke joyously to her son who was more interested in his anime than her good news.

"Remel, turn that off we have something to say," continued Adira.

Remel paused his laptop.

"We're getting married!" she exclaimed, whilst waving her engagement ring in the corner of Remel's peripheral vision.

"Congratulations," he sighed before returning to the episode.

It was clear that Adira had lost her son to the emotions that he grappled with internally. She and Asa stood worryingly behind him trying to find the right words to say. Remel too yearned for the ability to express himself and all of his troubles, but he failed to find any possible way to do so. Instead, quiet filled the room. Asa and Adira's presence gave Remel a sense of discomfort. Their relationship felt like an insult to his father, but he couldn't be angry at his mother for being able to move on.

Remel needed to run away. In that moment of awkward silence, as Remel searched for an escape from whatever factor it was that stood in the way of fluid conversation, he saw an envelope on the floor. It was a usual white envelope: rectangular, not large in size, and stamped in the corner, yet Remel was taken aback by its existence. For some odd reason, he needed to pick it up and analyse it as if he had been commanded to do so. The envelope was entitled to him. Literally. He felt no shock or surprise for somehow he had known that the envelope was his from the second he had laid eyes on it. Remel ripped it open with the urgency of a wild animal devouring its prey. Asa and Adira watched from the corner of the room, unable to understand what was going on. A folded piece of A4 paper was inside, almost blank, aside from a small typed note which read: 'Fire 1700'.

The scent of liberty hovered through the air. Remel, the inquisitive, ran past the couple, booted down the front door without being interrupted by any security guards and ran with the letter. He ran with an ignited spirit away from the unforgiving fury he had felt against Adira and the constitutions which had been put in place to keep him imprisoned in Asa's asylum. People on the streets dodged and danced nimbly to avoid bumping into the young man sprinting in the middle of the pavement like a starving cheetah with a pack of deer in sight. Within an hour of unmatched stamina and speed, Remel found himself in front of Rasharn's old house side by side with a tall man (around 6 foot 4) with a long overcoat and an iron mask. The man wore a small silver necklace, which had the word Leroy on it, underneath a white, slim fitted shirt. Both Remel and Keys looked at what once was a family home.

"Destruction," Keys sighed.

Remel nodded his head. He hadn't really understood why Keys had said it but he saw the word's relevance. They had destroyed each other, their own family and their home. Their tale was a mirror of the broken world of violence and misery that Remel used to inhabit.

"We have a lot to do," Keys stated.

And they flew.

*****

Epilogue
Chapter 1
(Twenty Years Later)

The demise of PC Connor.

The room was silent and void of light. The brick red floors were kept hidden by the blanket of dust that slept over it. Occasionally, the layer of dust was pierced by the drops of blood dripping from Juliana's lip. She was tied to a chair by the ankles, waist and wrists. If she could move, she wouldn't have hesitated to murder her captor regardless of her relationship with him. Her black eye only barely allowed her to see him as he entered into the room.

"Juliana, I don't want to hurt you. I've already explained to you that all of this pain is self-inflicted. You just need to help me so we can get through all of this... Where is he?" whispered PC Connor as he bent down to his daughter's level and caressed her cheek as he spoke.

She mustered all of the phlegm in her throat and spat in her father's face with scarlet red blood that encapsulated a fraction of the hatred she had in her. This was the ultimate act of disrespect. Damien Connor drew his hand back, ready to strike his daughter, but he paused an inch away from her face to show that he had restraint. He took a step back, wiped his face and began to stroll around the dark room which murmured tones of evil. He went through his plan over and over again like a psychotic perfectionist. Juliana was disgusted by the sight of him and wished only to make him suffer for everything he had done to her.

They both waited.

Juliana broke the patient silence that ensued with uncontrolled laughter. She stared at her father as she did so. He was proud of her bravery. She had definitely acquired it from him.

"You may think you know what you're getting involved with, but everything you've done over all this time, everything you've tried to force me to be a part of and everything you've pretended to be is finished once my husband comes, Damien."

PC Connor turned to his daughter and corrected her use of his first name. He was her father and not her friend. She corrected him by reminding him that fathers did not kidnap their daughters to find their enemies. He noted her point.

A gunshot-like sound was heard in the distance.

A knock came at the door of the room. This was him. Damien's plan was now coming into fruition. Damien opened the door for his nemesis who was dressed in a long overcoat that stopped just above his knees with slim-fit, black trousers and a white buttoned shirt. The visitor's face was decorated with an iron mask. PC Connor took a step back as he pulled his gun out of his pocket and aimed it for his nemesis' face. The masked man darted around the room like a ninja in order to evade the line of fire of PC Connor's gun. In the hope that he could luckily shoot his prey, Damien, the stone cold killer, shot aimlessly. A bullet flew towards Juliana. The gun, which had a silencer on the end, had let off its bullet without warning so Juliana had no time to react. The masked man pointed at the bullet, and it stopped in its tracks: he had telekinesis—the ability to move things with his mind. The masked man proved that he could also do so at supersonic speeds as he sent the bullet away from Juliana speedily, narrowly missing Damien's face.

The masked visitor lunged at PC Connor as if he had just flown out of the barrel of a cannon. He landed heavily on the officer and started punching him in the face repeatedly whilst telling Juliana to run away. She thought to ask how she could do so whilst she was imprisoned by the ropes on her chair, but she felt him loosening the knots using his telekinesis. She managed to crawl slowly. The officer grabbed his assailant by the throat like two pigeons taking their food in vicious hunger. The masked man used his powers to loosen the officer's grip and continued to pound him in the centre of his face. PC Connor left his blood all over his adversary's fists. The masked man wished to continue his attack as he was consumed by an anger for everything he had done to his wife, but he was able stop himself.

Once PC Connor had realised that there was no hope for him to complete the two pivotal parts of his plan, which were unmask the masked man and kill him after doing so, he took a small blue pill out of his pocket, chewed it and died quickly. The masked man flew his wife, Juliana back home.

As they flew, Juliana looked down at her husband's lips. Not only did she long to kiss them as soon as she arrived in the comfort of her home, but she also wished to know the long awaited story of the scar on his lip that she had been waiting to hear for the past 20 years.

Epilogue
Chapter 2

Remel Brathwaite, the CEO of the multi-million pound Revolución software industries, is at home with his wife. Both of them are recovering from injury. The date is October 29th.

On the windowsill, in a cage, seemingly trapped by glass, yet free to escape through an open hatch in the top corner, lay a caterpillar in downward slumber, hidden within the confines of its cocoon. A vast array of flowers and plants sat on display around the room, creating an immersive showcase of colour and radiance. Rays of sun pierced through the living room, intruding the couple's privacy as Juliana's cheeks blushed a light fuschia under the touch of Remel's soft kiss. She was sat next to him, watching a movie on television whilst the two of them thought deeply about what had just happened and its implications on the rest of their lives. It was a bittersweet victory that they attempted to relish in joyfully before considering the effects of.

Juliana stood up, kissed her husband on the lips and told him she was going to turn the kettle on. This was married life. Remel chuckled to himself and questioned when he had transformed into his current state. Reminiscing on his past as a lonely rebel not quite fuelled by anger but more so by curious waywardness, the millionaire sighed pensively. The doorbell rang. The sound of the ring was a high-pitched melody which resembled a syncopated and slowed down combination of traditional afro beat and jazz. Remel opened the door to the sight of a vicar dressed smartly in a black shirt, a clerical collar and a suit. The vicar looked at Remel with an expression of loss and nostalgia. In silence, the two men looked at each other for a couple of seconds. For them it felt like an eternity. However, in a sudden burst of realisation, Remel recognised the vicar and understood his expression of loss and nostalgia. Remel's guest was Rasharn White. He was still chubby, slightly taller and visibly tired from age. Remel's guest allowed his eyes to wander around the sight of the home: an open plan 8-bedroom house decorated with the most beautiful of bonsais, orchids and flowering money trees. From the outside, Remel's home was a big yet simple display of bricks. It was only when the door was opened that its beauties could be shown.

"Can we go for a walk?" asked Rasharn, the vicar, breaking their silence.

Looking behind him and seeing that his wife was still in the kitchen, Remel left the house and closed the door behind him without saying anything. The two of them strolled casually in the busy town centre for several minutes before Rasharn began to speak. The silence was more necessary than awkward. Years of memories began to surge between them, making it difficult to begin the conversation.

"I gave my life to Christ around twenty years ago. It was just that day after my house burnt down… I realised that that life wasn't for me. We were twisted individuals, ruining ourselves, sinning beyond remorse. I think you realised that early on. That's why you are the way you are now and I went through everything I did. I feel like everything happens for a reason you know. But some things… we just can't explain. I've been praying for answers from God. And he led me to you. Of course, it wasn't easy finding your house but today I did it. I need to know… What was it exactly that happened on the day of that fight, Remel?"

Rasharn had no time for introductions. His hair, prematurely grey and balding at the top, shouted of his desperation. Meanwhile, Remel looked just as old as he did on the day of his televised speech. As he stroked his chin and frowned his brows uneasily, Rasharn's thoughts screamed of a longing to know the truth. Remel knew exactly the fight in question; that was when it all went wrong for Rasharn. However, for Remel, that day was like a point of salvation. He sighed, mirroring the cold winds of the deceptively bright autumn day. Remel had been going to church infrequently over the past few years, slowly undoing his years of mistrust in Christianity.

"'For I know the plans I have for you,' declares the Lord, 'plans to prosper you and not to harm you, plans to give you hope and a future.' You know that one right? Jeremiah 29:11. It's funny because I don't really believe in that nonsense. Things don't happen for a reason. We aren't robots, pre-programmed to make our life choices. Our futures are not planned for us. But me and you weren't really made for that life that we used to live. We were made for *this*: the present day. It doesn't really make sense but that day of the fight, before we all went home casually as if nothing too serious had happened, we were offered an alternative, a new opportunity, an..." Remel's voice trailed off as he lost himself in an ocean of thoughts.

"An escape?" offered Rasharn, also in deep thought, growing satisfied by Remel's vague revelation.

Remel nodded his head silently. The two continued to speak about trivial things. It was a reunion. Once they had finished, Rasharn shook Remel's hand firmly, offering him words of blessing. Remel politely acknowledged Rasharn's words and left him at the bus stop before flying home to Juliana. He arrived to his door and opened it to see his wife stood before him, grateful to see him return.

"Who was that?" she asked.

"Just an old friend," replied Remel, taking his seat back in front of the movie which had been paused for him.

Juliana presented him a small assortment of snacks that she gathered from the kitchen next to two cups of tea. She sat next to him. A light blue butterfly flew towards the couple from nowhere. Remel, the intuitive, turned his head to the windowsill and looked at the empty glass cage. The caterpillar had freed itself from his glass cage and spread its wings.

Juliana followed what Remel was looking at and they both smiled peacefully.